The Mischief Makers

By the same author

THE CONSPIRATORS
A COOL DAY FOR KILLING
THE HARDLINERS
THE BITTER HARVEST
THE PROTECTORS
THE KINSMEN
THE SCORPION'S TAIL
YESTERDAY'S ENEMY
THE POISON PEOPLE
VISA TO LIMBO
THE MEDIAN LINE
THE MONEY MEN

The
Mischief Makers

William Haggard

WALKER AND COMPANY
NEW YORK

c.1

SUSPENSE

First published in the United States of America in 1982 by the Walker Publishing Company, Inc.

ISBN: 0-8027-5471-6

Library of Congress Catalog Card Number: 81-71418

Printed in the United States of America

10 9 8 7 6 5 4 3 2 1   **BL** AUG 5 '82

Chapter 1

The old man pulled his beard reflectively. Of late it had started to speckle handsomely but it was dyed to its original black. He preferred to look what in fact he was, a virile and still formidable man. He had fourteen daughters but only eight sons, and in this he considered that fate had been unkind. But his latest and youngest wife was pregnant and the *hakim* had assured him confidently that the signs and portents were unmistakably male. He thought of her with an affectionate smile for she hadn't concealed a surprise which had flattered him. If she'd suspected that she might have to coax and wheedle, the lady had been gravely mistaken. Mistaken and entirely delighted. Her husband smiled in his splendid beard. Once again a duty had also been pleasurable.

He fell into a mid-morning reverie. He had come a long way since he'd left his village, speaking no tongue but his Berber dialect. He didn't love the French but was content to serve them, as his ancestors had for more than a century. He still had his great-grandfather's captured swords, an artillery officer's useless appurtenances. They fitted together in a fine leather scabbard and the hilts were of superlative workmanship. His grandfather had looted them, fighting the heathen Russians in the Crimea. He himself had risen to under-officer and gone back to his village to live on his pension. He had expected to live in a modest dignity, since his youth if not his vigour was now behind him.

In the event he had done no such thing, for the War of Liberation had snatched him into its maelstrom with the rest. Not a gentleman's war, he reflected sourly: neither side had observed the accepted rules. Prisoners tortured and women raped, one of his own daughters among them. Not decently raped which he might have forgotten but raped with the extreme of dishonour. They had deflowered her with the neck of a beer bottle, offensive to any father alive and to a Muslim an act of utter barbarity. Later she had committed suicide.

Behind his beard his mouth set grimly. He was sworn on his

father's grave to avenge her and he'd gone up in the world since he'd served the French. His country had won its independence but the men of the coastal Tell had betrayed it. He and his brothers, the clans, the hillmen, had come down from their mountains and taken over.

By God, he thought now, they had needed luck, and Allah in His wisdom had granted it. He remembered that they'd been no more than a rabble – World War One rifles, ancient bayonets, even pikes. He hadn't overly feared the army for they were still mostly men of his own strong blood and, like many civilians, were disenchanted. But the air force was Frenchified – worse, it was Arabised – and the moment his men left their hills and forests it could mow them down in the open like cattle.

Some of that moment's tension returned to him. The first aircraft had come over and dived. Some but not all had fired. Men had fallen. There hadn't been time for total panic for the second wave was ten seconds behind the first. This too had dived but it hadn't fired. He had even seen a pilot waving. He had gathered his rabble together marching on, and next morning at dawn he had seen the tank. It was flying a flag of truce and he let it come on. He couldn't in fact have stopped it if he had wished. From it descended the Commander-in-Chief, a kinsman who spoke the old man's dialect. They parleyed, shook hands, and marched on to the capital.

Now he was the respected President of a ramshackle but viable state. But he had still to avenge a dishonoured daughter. He had made his plan and chosen his instrument but he was getting impatient with Michael Henshawe.

He ran his country in the only way known to him, as a feudal estate with himself as overlord. There were ministers and even a parliament, technicians to do what was nowadays necessary, but real power was held in the hands of his family. He sent for the head of his Private Bureau. Naturally he was one of his sons. He had been to an English school and was clever but his father's will came first and always would.

"Abdel! Good morning."

"Good morning, father." He knelt to receive his blessing.

"Any news from that Henshawe?"

6

"No, not much. He says only that he has made some progress."

"After all that money – made some progress?"

Abdelaziz might have said with truth that he would much have preferred a proven professional, but instead he nodded and stayed standing patiently. He himself was by now a grandfather but he didn't sit down until invited to.

But he was going to risk the old man's anger by showing a discreet dissent, for in this matter of avenging his half-sister he thought his father was mildly obsessive. This was the strongest word he allowed himself and even that was a secret betrayal. Nevertheless, it *was* an obsession. The rapist was dead and the matter ended. He'd been a French Legionnaire but not a Frenchman, evidently a very low animal. He had also been a very bad soldier. Later he'd tried to desert and been shot. A plan to bring down his country in ruins was, in Abdel's opinion, an over-reaction.

But to say so would be worse than unfilial since his father's rages could still shake the bravest. He approached the matter obliquely, saying:

"It is not for me to doubt your intention, but I have been wondering whether your method is basically right. Might we not learn from a certain neighbour?"

"Certainly not." The old man was contemptuous. Several hundred miles to the east was an Arab (though other Arabs hotly denied it) whose apparent hobby was stirring up trouble wherever the chance of trouble offered. He gave money to the I.R.A., to the P.L.O., to terrorist gangs in Western Germany with hyphenated names and untidy habits. And he did so from the worst motives possible, for the man was an intellectual upstart, dreaming his dream of the resurgence of Islam. But *jihads* were plainly out of date. Moreover he was some sort of idealist, whatever that word might mean at this moment. The old man wanted a decent revenge but this Johnny-come-lately was blown tight with abstractions. He was an international nuisance and probably mad.

Abdelaziz was intelligent and could unerringly read his father's mind. Who said surprisingly mildly:

"Speak on."

"I was wondering whether the I.R.A. .... I mean if we switched the guns to them ..."

His father shook his head at once. "I think you are seeing the politics wrongly. If Ulster sank under the sea tomorrow many Englishmen would sigh with relief. It's been a thorn in their flesh for quite a time and retaining it also costs them money. If the Republic invaded they'd be bound to resist, but that isn't likely so on they muddle. But organised risings in England itself –"

"I take the point."

"I hadn't finished. For nothing on this earth would persuade me to give bullet or bomb to men who kill children." The old man spat in his handkerchief neatly.

His father was being exceptionally amenable and Abdel risked what he otherwise wouldn't have. "They're savages but at least they're white."

The old man took it without surprise. "Meaning that Henshawe's connections are not?"

"That's what I meant."

"And again I think you've got it wrong. I don't pretend to be wholly unprejudiced – God made us as He saw fit to do so – but when forty per cent of these blacks are British born ... That would appeal to my sense of humour. I have one, you know, though I don't often show it."

... You have one indeed and it's wholly your own. Unfashionable? Yes, but not only unfashionable. Let us call it sardonic and leave it at that.

The President sent for strong black coffee. "Did you know that your maternal grandmother was rather more than half a Turk?"

"I have heard my mother say so – yes."

"It was she who gave me a taste for this poison. Now I cannot live without it."

Abdelaziz drank his coffee slowly for he had news to deliver. It wasn't good. "I'm glad you sent for me. I have something to tell you."

"About Henshawe? But you said you had nothing."

"No, not about Henshawe."

"Then what?" It was sharp.

"It's news about Maoui."

"Oh him! He's negligible."

8

Maoui was their ambassador in London. The old man roundly disliked all diplomats, despising their shadowy trade amongst half-men, but Maoui was an experienced professional, and though he had served a corrupt regime he had been left at St James's to work his time out.

"He's certainly wet but he's also treacherous."

"How?"

"He's planning to double-cross us."

"How again?"

"Those arms we send go in through the Bag."

"Of course they do. How else could we send them?" It was spoken without a hint of embarrassment.

"Henshawe hides them in a place in the country."

"Till he's ready to use them."

"That was the basic plan."

"You said 'was'."

"Maoui's planning to hand them over to the police."

Abdelaziz had expected an outburst. None came. Instead his father said almost gently:

"Better tell the whole story."

Abdelaziz did so. He spoke deliberately, spacing the sentences, for his father's mind was less quick than it had been. "Maoui would like to stay on in England. He has saved a good deal and would marry his mistress, who was once a very rich man's wife. But he'd have to be accepted first – I think the jargon word is 'asylum'. That's something they grant less easily nowadays but they probably would as the price of those guns. Asylum and perhaps protection."

The old man said dourly: "He would certainly need it." He reflected, then added briskly: "How do you know this?"

"It came from his secretary. Maoui has been a little careless."

"This secretary is one of your people?"

"Of course."

The President nodded; he understood. There were embassies in England's capital where the real boss might be the cultural attaché. His own was not one of these, or not yet, but it didn't surprise him that his own Private Bureau had a man there who would report a defection. He said to his son:

9

"And now?"

"I came to ask."

The old man thought it over carefully. Two things must be done and both were simple, but even simple orders were useless without being sure of the means to carry them out. His country was run as a family fief, but though nepotic it wasn't yet soft in the muscle. This son, the head of his Private Bureau, had had to be good at his trade to get to the top.

"Would you care to go back to England?"

"Not much." Abdel had been to school there but unfruitfully.

"Have you anyone who could deal with Maoui and also put the spurs into Henshawe? He has taken a lot for so little progress."

"I have a dozen men who could deal with Maoui but Henshawe is a different problem. I agree he's been slow to produce results, but I'm obliged to say that he may have difficulties – the difficulties of a white man trying to rouse blacks. I'd have preferred a man of greater experience but we simply didn't have one available. Henshawe's eaten by hate or he wouldn't be working for us, but I wish he had had some practical training."

"Is he practical enough to move those weapons? From where they are now, I mean, and hide them again?"

"I would hope he could manage that. As he must."

"Then I am sending you to London at once as a counsellor in Maoui's embassy."

Abdelaziz didn't like it but bowed. The old man couldn't last for ever and when he died there'd be a savage power struggle. Abdelaziz didn't want to be President but he liked his job and intended to keep it. "And Maoui?" he enquired.

"Ah yes. Do you know when he plans to betray us?"

"Not yet."

The President shrugged. "It is really irrelevant. Provided the weapons have been re-hidden. Can you leave today?"

"If those are your wishes." Abdel hesitated, then repeated: "And Maoui?"

"Maoui is a traitor."

"I understand."

When his son had gone the old man closed his eyes. His daughter, he thought – his favourite daughter. She'd been

10

fighting with the men and they hadn't touched her. Then she'd been captured and an animal had. He saw her as she'd returned when they let her go. Disarmed of course, and doubly dishonoured.

A shudder shook him ... With a beer bottle! The deed was intolerable. There was only one God and He mustn't be mocked. Any one of the Faithful must see that He wasn't.

Jack Pallant had been much surprised for he wasn't accustomed to calls from ambassadors. Sometimes he saw smooth first secretaries who came to delate on men they disliked. Pallant heard them politely and sent them away, since mostly their information was gossip, and when it was not he often knew it already. But an ambassador was a sharp rise in the stakes.

He wondered what they now were; he couldn't guess. He was head of the Security Executive but his background was Very Senior Policeman, and he lacked the panache of Colonel Charles Russell in whose hot seat he now sat as best he could. For he knew that he was a stop-gap choice. There was going to be a General Election, and if the Left won they'd have him out at once, slipping in some stooge of their own, whereas if it went Right he was not quite their man. It would probably be some retired major-general.

He made his first decision easily. He would hear this ambassador out with patience but if the matter went beyond him, as he suspected it would, he would take it to Charles Russell for advice. As a policeman he had been close to Russell and Russell still had the political know-how, the international reputation.

The next decision was not so straightforward. It would be unthinkable to see this man alone. Anything said could be twisted wickedly, or the interview might be some sort of trap. He could, of course, tape it but that might be dangerous. It was better to have a living witness ... Who? The obvious choice was the officer on the case, James Bullen. This Maoui was bringing in arms in the Bag but beyond that the evidence stopped uncomfortably. There was nothing to show they'd been handed out, no sudden spurt of violent action by any of the obvious recipients. So the presumption, and that was all it was, was that these weapons had somewhere been hidden away till whatever the plan be was ripe.

11

At that sort of thing James Bullen was excellent. He was a paper-man and an excellent listener who might pick up some nuance which Pallant had missed, then he'd sit up all night till the pattern came out right. Pallant thought of him with a real respect; he would have hated to lose him and once nearly had. If he'd married Barbara Rhys-Harte he'd have had to resign. Happily that hadn't happened.

So Bullen, then, but that wasn't enough. If this interview went as Pallant feared, it might lead to the need for urgent action and Bullen wasn't a field-man – quite the reverse. He was scholarly with a first-class brain but in the rough stuff would be entirely useless. He had never been trained in the arts of violence, and Pallant was inclined to suspect that secretly he resented this.

Then who else but William Wilberforce Smith should know of any new development? He'd been one of Charles Russell's inspired appointments and had proved himself outside the office; he had been to a public school and had money; he thought of himself as an establishment Englishman.

The fact that his skin was black was irrelevant and it wasn't inconceivable that one day he might sit in Pallant's chair.

So the three men rose to receive his excellency and waited to sit down till he did. He showed no surprise at a West Indian's presence. The old man had been wise to leave him *en poste* since he was experienced in the ways of the West. He showed no surprise but observed acutely. Willy's quiet, expensive clothes said good taste; his superbly polished shoes said discipline. The accent said nothing at all. There wasn't one.

They chatted of trifles till Pallant was ready, then:

"What can I do for you?"

"I haven't come for a favour but to offer a deal."

"Interesting," Jack Pallant said.

"I am hoping you will find it so." Maoui looked at Pallant and made up his mind; he was going to play it straight down the middle. "I imagine you have a file on me."

"A question you know I cannot answer."

"The answer I expected, sir, but whether or not you have is irrelevant. I'd be a fool to suppose that you hadn't found out that we've been smuggling in weapons in the Bag."

"May I take that as an admission?"

"If that is the word you prefer – by all means."

"Then where do we go from here?"

"I will tell you." Maoui accepted a cup of tea. "I would like to marry in this country and settle here."

"Then haven't you come to quite the wrong office?"

"If you're thinking of the Home Office – no. Naturally I have contacts there but again I'd be very greatly surprised if they didn't know I'd been breaking the rules. It's very unlikely they'd agree to my staying."

"Then where do I come in?"

"As a go-between."

"Between yourself and the Home Office?"

"Yes. Exactly. You too must have friends there."

Jack Pallant smiled his saurian smile for he was a man who liked to use words with precision. He did know a man in the top-heavy Home Office with whom he had once worked successfully, but he wasn't in any sense his friend. So he allowed the smile but asked the next question.

"Why should they listen to me if not to you?"

"They would listen if you came bearing gifts."

Pallant was more than a little surprised for he hadn't considered this man a fool. His surprise was showing and the ambassador noticed it. He said on a note of irritation:

"If you're thinking of money forget it at once. If I thought I could bribe a secretary of state I would approach him without a broker between us."

"Then, for the second time, where do I come in?"

"I spoke of a deal."

"I am here to listen."

"If *you* were to tell the Home Office that I had done your country a very great service they would find it hard to refuse me asylum." He saw that all three men were now alert. Bullen especially was listening intently.

"As an abstract proposition I must agree."

"Then I will make it something more than abstract. If you will give me your word you will press my case I will tell you where those arms are hidden."

There was an astonished silence which Bullen broke. "That might not be enough," he said.

They're good at their job, the ambassador thought. They're pressing me. They know their business.

Pallant said quietly: "Yes. I agree."

"May I ask what more you would need to help me?"

"What the arms were for. Who was running your plan here."

Maoui thought it over, decided. He wanted passionately to stay in England. "What the plan was I cannot tell you – I do not know. But I know the name of the man we were using. Have I your word you will press my case if I give you both location and name?"

It was Pallant's turn to think with care for it was the biggest decision he'd ever been asked to make. If all went well he'd have pulled off a coup but if something went wrong he'd be out of the window. He said at last:

"With reluctance. But yes."

Maoui took from his pocket an ordinance survey map, talking more easily now; he was over his fence. "I've never understood map references but I've marked the spot in ink as you see. It's an old disused pillbox, kept locked against tramps, the sort you built against invasion by Hitler. Naturally the lock has been changed." He felt in a pocket. "Here is the key."

"*The* key?"

"What was that?"

"Hasn't your man another?"

"Yes."

"I see." Pallant had gone as stiff as steel. "And now the man's name, please."

"Michael Henshawe."

"That rings a faint bell."

"I thought it was possible."

Pallant had risen first but Maoui held him. "Is the bargain understood?"

"It is. Is there any further business?"

"None."

"In that case I will see you to your car."

Pallant went down with Maoui and showed him out. The car had a CD plate but a small one. Pallant knew it was unnecessary

14

since the police had the numbers of top diplomats' cars. But there it was in its stark vulgarity. At least, Pallant thought, it's discreetly small. The Gulf States flaunted things the size of flags.

"Good evening, your excellency."

"Good evening, sir. I wish you good hunting." He didn't hold out his hand and Pallant was glad. Men who sold out their masters were not his favourites.

He returned to Willy Smith and Bullen. "Well?" he enquired.

"Not well at all." They had spoken together and Pallant laughed.

"Have we a file on this Henshawe? The name does stir the dust a bit."

"You could call it a precautionary file, since up to this he's done nothing to interest us except to have the sort of background which does."

"Please send it up, I want to soak in it. I foresee every sort of snag and perhaps a snare. But one thing we'll have to do at once and that's check on those arms – are they really there?" He turned to Willy Smith. "Can do?"

"I'll go tonight."

"Tonight?"

"Why not?" Willy was consulting his diary. "There's a moon," he said. "May I use your telephone?" He returned from it, apparently satisfied. "The weather people don't think there'll be cloud."

"Get a larger-scale map if you're moving by night."

"I'd thought of that," Willy said politely.

. . . He's competent, all right. He thinks of things.

"Then the best of luck."

Pallant turned away to James Bullen. A shadow had passed across his face and Pallant was an observant man. He put a hand on Bullen's shoulder gently. "There'll be plenty of work for you too," he said.

He guessed as he spoke that the words were a lie but in the event they were a sort of epitaph.

His excellency was in very good heart. The sudden posting of a non-career counsellor had surprised and, for a moment, frightened

15

him, but he had rationalised away his first alarm. After all, he'd been able to tell himself, Abdelaziz was the old man's son and when he died there'd be a merciless struggle. Abdelaziz could be one of the strugglers, one with a very good chance of success, but perhaps the old man preferred someone else and was getting Abdel out of the way. To groom him for an ambassadorship would serve that end and also another: it would generously provide for a son of his loins. Occasionally a faint doubt nagged – the reasoning was unsupported – but at this moment Maoui put it behind him since he didn't wish to spoil his luncheon.

He was lunching with his mistress, his future wife. She'd been divorced in circumstances which some had thought questionable, but her husband had been a wealthy man, the lady's solicitors sharp and ruthless, and her husband had been bled white to get rid of her. Maoui, over the years, had been prudent and together they'd have an ample income. They had discussed it and agreed entirely. They would buy a little house in London and there they would entertain as they wished, not the boring diplomatic round but people of the sort they both liked. Maoui had been to a French university where he'd got helplessly hooked on modern painting, and his mistress had friends in the world of letters, the sort whose books were reviewed very seriously, but who needed inherited money to live on. Of course, the old man would be furiously angry – Maoui was going to need a bodyguard. But not, he rather fancied, for long. Whoever stepped into the President's chair would have other things to think about, including a vicious and half-mad neighbour, than the pursuance of a private vendetta. Moreover, though he hadn't been told it, Maoui had guessed the old man's plan and believed it to be a plain non-starter. A white man raising a black revolution! The shot wasn't on, except as a fluke.

He had been born in the solemn mummery of diplomacy. Of what happened in real life he was ignorant.

He put his thoughts from his head and took a drink. His embassy was forbidden alcohol but Maoui took a drink when he felt like one. Not the hard stuff, he hadn't come round to that, but he'd acquired other things in France than a taste for Abstracts. He liked the solid wines of the Côtes du Rhône and at this moment was on

16

Beaumes de Venise. He bought it at a multiple grocer but his excellency was not a wine snob.

Presently he looked at his watch. He rang for his car and went downstairs to it. The driver opened the door and stepped back. There was the crack of a shot and Maoui staggered. He fell heavily in the gutter. He was dead.

Chapter 2

Pallant read Henshawe's file with attention, conscious that although he had spoken of soaking himself he was merely reading a story line by line. For Henshawe wasn't the kind of man with whom a good policeman had daily dealings. He wasn't a professional agent, but from this story he might be equally dangerous. Jack Pallant made his mind up quickly. He would send this file to Colonel Charles Russell who would read between the lines and understand. Understand, Pallant thought, not merely absorb. He called James Bullen and said to him pleasantly:

"A first-class job but I simply don't mesh on it. So take it round yourself to Charles Russell."

"Very well, sir. But of course it's irregular."

"I know perfectly well it's quite irregular, but Charles Russell has what I haven't – experience. I don't understand what comes out of Ireland and Russell does. Add to that that he sat in this chair illustriously." Pallant looked at a clock. "But telephone first. He sometimes takes a nap in the afternoon."

James Bullen's call did in fact disturb Russell but he dressed at once and waited eagerly. He was somewhere in his sixties now but still active and as sharp as a razor. He had been head of the Executive in the days of its undoubted greatness and it flattered him when Pallant still sent him files. He didn't send him the boring ones and sometimes a file could spill over to action. Russell's nostrils very slightly flared, the old war horse was scenting the distant battle.

He opened the door to a man unknown to him. "James Bullen," he said, "and I've come from the office." He was carrying a substantial briefcase and Russell noticed that it was chained to his wrist.

"Come in," Russell said. "Will you take a drink?"

"A little early, thank you, sir." He began to unfasten the briefcase deliberately.

The refusal did not surprise Charles Russell since it was indeed rather early for drinking. What surprised him was the man's appearance – receding hair and heavy horn spectacles, the quintessential backroom boy. He had been hoping for something a little more lively, even for William Wilberforce Smith. Pallant knew that he had recruited Willy in the face of several ponderous headshakings; he knew that Willy adored Charles Russell; and he knew that he had once saved his life. Willy's skin was the colour of coal in the rain but the appointment had been a roaring success. For Willy was third generation in England with an enviable education and income, and as Russell had guessed before appointing him he thought of himself as an upper-middle-class Englishman. Russell had looked forward to seeing him but he hid his disappointment politely. He nodded at the massive file, asking:

"How long have I got to read through that?"

"Could you finish it by this evening?"

"That urgent?"

"Mr Pallant seems to think so."

"I'll do my best."

Bullen picked up his hat. "Then Mr Pallant will ring at nine."

He took his leave.

Russell settled in a chair with the file and in three pages it had set him alight. For this was country he knew and understood. The Henshawes had been in Southern Ireland for more centuries than they cared to remember, living on lands which were not their own, either granted to them by an alien king or in many cases simply stolen; and as the centuries had slipped by sleepily they had seldom, if ever, taken a bride from the race which lived in the world outside their gates. They had married into their own close caste and always they had stayed bitterly protestant. Today they were doomed like all other colonists, like the English in what was now Zimbabwe, like the French who had lost their war in Algeria.

This was the background and also Russell's own. It could be happy enough in its fading way till the bailiffs came and the roof fell in on you, but Michael Henshawe's childhood had not been happy. He was the son of an ageing man's second wife, a frivolous socially-minded woman who had run through what little money was left in entertaining which she couldn't afford. When his father died the crash came after him: the estate was bankrupt, the house near a ruin. By local standards it had never been big, but there were some fine things in it and these were sold. They paid the mortgages but left little over. The land was snapped up by local farmers.

But though there was very little left over there'd been enough to educate Michael Henshawe. He had been sent to an English public school where he'd been miserable but had kept his head down. The school had been a second-class one and, being so, had pretended hard that it was really in the upper bracket. Its prides had been its squash and athletics, both attritive pastimes which reflected its ethos. Henshawe had been a passable cricketer but he wasn't any good at athletics, and the boy who really ran this school was one who was called the captain of sports. He had taken a dislike to Henshawe and had the power to make his life a misery.

But Henshawe had survived successfully till his time had come to go to Sandhurst. His feet had been naturally set in the path which generations of impoverished Irish had beaten into the British army. He would get his commission and somehow live on his pay.

He had done neither since he had failed to pass Sandhurst. He had failed to pass off the square and had been put back a term. Then he'd failed again and been asked to leave.

Russell nodded for he was sympathetic. He had been through Sandhurst himself and had loathed it, the bawling drill sergeants and the dandified adjutant, a man from a regiment his own thought stuffy. Of course it had changed a good deal from his own time but he still thought the system archaic and wasteful. Some boys could survive in a walking dream and others like himself decided that if drill were all that important they would excel. Michael Henshawe had not and they'd squeezed him out. Enough to embitter any boy, and one with Michael Henshawe's background . . .

Russell read on: it got steadily worse. There'd been a job in a bank and then second disaster. For Henshawe was living beyond his means and one day his till had been two hundred short. Almost certainly on some lunatic impulse but the bank had decided to make an example, talking of the fiduciary relationship and if banks weren't safe from pilfering who was? It had pressed the case up to the hilt and beyond it. Henshawe had collected a swingeing sentence. It had been reduced on appeal but not by much.

So how was he living now? Not too badly. He had a job on a south London paper which paid him a pittance for writing well, but he also had another income which was suspected to come from a foreign state. He was living with a girl called Rhys-Harte who worked in an organisation called FAAR.

Up to now Charles Russell had read with sympathy but now he allowed a sardonic chuckle ... The Foundation for the Advancement of African Rights. FAAR. Add a T, Russell thought, and the acronym would be perfect. For they all of them had joined its board, the bishop of Crondal, Lord Welcome-Wills, Mrs Alderney Cohn, the usual clique of them, the decaying fat on the body politic. They protested, they wrote indignant letters, they lobbied in the forests where no bird stirred. But they didn't achieve a thing that mattered. The whole set-up was so patently futile that it could only be a front for another.

Russell saw that he had two pages left but had already formed his own opinion. It would be interesting to hold the last paragraphs, to see if they confirmed what he thought. He put the file aside and poured a drink.

It hadn't been an unusual story – Russell had seen too many, much the same. A man was broken, went sourly bitter, but he didn't often take money from foreign states. Instead he joined the humanist agonisers, an iconoclast without a hammer; he thought in terms of an unjust society which it was his duty to reform if he could. Without violence of course, since all violence was evil. But Henshawe might have a simpler target, the English, John Bull, the ancestral enemy. By definition he was an Anglo-Irishman but he might well have turned his back on the 'Anglo'. It had happened before and always disastrously.

Neat, Russell thought, but so far unproven. Just one thing would establish it though, or would establish it to his agnate experience. Perhaps it was on the file. He went back to it.

The words sprang out of the page unequivocally. Henshawe had become a Catholic and Russell knew what that meant precisely: it was the final turning his back on his past, the ultimate cocking a snook at his ancestry. He didn't appear to be a good one, for once

22

admitted he'd never been near a Mass. Russell smiled as he thought of some good priest's dilemma. Henshawe would have done his homework, he'd have had all the answers correct and pat, but any experienced priest must have felt a doubt. In which case he would have asked his superior and Russell could guess the answer easily. It would be error to admit a sham but a sin to refuse if the man were genuine. Charles Russell laughed. They had it all ways.

He went back to his chair with his half-finished drink since he now knew what he would say to Pallant. He would say that Henshawe could fizzle out like a squib but could also be extremely dangerous. When that sort of man went sour he *was* dangerous. Russell couldn't defend him but nor could he blame. He had almost been there once himself when he had been thrown on the scrapheap as a sop to the Left.

He didn't often talk to himself but now he said with a sort of humility: "There but for the Grace of God go I. We're all the same, we English from Ireland. Either we escape or we've had it." As he had escaped, he reflected. Not too badly. He had made colonel from a first-class regiment, then a great reputation as the head of Security; he had served the Bull and done so honourably. And if he hadn't? Then one of two things. Either go back to his brother's house, teaching *nouveaux riches* West Germans polo, or else he would have followed Henshawe.

There but for the good Bull's grace go I.

Abdelaziz was his father's son but he wouldn't have been the head of the Bureau if he hadn't been through the mill successfully. He cleaned the rifle carefully, then locked it in the embassy strong-room. He washed his hands and sent for a taxi; he was going to call on Michael Henshawe and he was going to do so perfectly openly. There wasn't as yet a reason not to. Later the contact might well be more difficult with Henshawe shadowed, his phone tapped, the rest of it. But for the moment he, Abdel, was out in the clear (except for a trifling matter of murder) and he had the professional's contempt for unnecessary precautions.

He knocked on the door and it opened at once. "We have met before in my father's country and I've been sent here with an urgent message."

"Then please come in." Henshawe opened the door. He was in shirt-sleeves and was wearing an apron. "Please sit down while I make myself tidy."

Abdel did so, looking round the flat. It wasn't the pad of an agent in fiction, but it was comfortable and reasonably clean. The bedroom door had been left wide open, and from where he sat he could see into it clearly. There was a double bed and a woman's nightdress. Abdelaziz permitted a smile. So in one respect at least it was running to form.

He could hear that Michael Henshawe was washing and he used the time to remember the story. He had just completed his prison sentence and was looking for another job but had first wanted to wash off the smell of prison. So he had come to Abdelaziz's country and there his father's car had knocked him down. Many men would simply have called doctor and ambulance but Abdel's father had old-fashioned standards. He had certainly called the doctor and ambulance but he had directed them to his private house. When you injured a man, that is by accident, you had a duty to do what you could to atone. Henshawe had had a broken leg and it had taken rather long to mend. The old man had been an attentive host and they had had French in common to reach understanding. Henshawe's was rather better than Abdel's father's.

At the time Abdelaziz had not much liked it, thinking a mutual lust for revenge was a frail foundation for a plan so ambitious as bringing down a still-powerful state. Now he wasn't so sure, for Michael Henshawe had changed. He had only seen him for thirty seconds but there was something about him that he had lacked before, a sort of assurance, an air of competence. It was true he was being extremely slow, but as Abdelaziz had warned his father, there might well be legitimate reasons for that. Meanwhile Michael Henshawe had clearly matured: the business of secret subversion had brought him on. The embittered boy was now an embittered man. That was good.

Henshawe returned wearing jacket and tie, still walking with a very faint limp. "I'm sorry I've had to keep you waiting. Normally my friend does the housework but this evening she isn't here. I apologise."

Abdel was quietly impressed: this was seemly. Good manners

proved nothing but were often a pointer. "I'm afraid I have come with very bad news."

"You mean the operation is off?" It had been spoken with a real disappointment and Abdel was again reassured.

"On the contrary, but it's still bad news." Henshawe said nothing and Abdelaziz went on. He told the tale of Maoui's shameless defection, ending matter-of-factly: "So. So naturally the man has been dealt with. If you wish to know it I killed him myself."

Michael Henshawe showed no sign of surprise and Abdel added another mark. And he asked a very sensible question:

"Do you think that Maoui also gave them my name?"

"I think we must assume that he certainly did."

"It could be important. The police or perhaps the Security Executive –" Abdelaziz was head of the Private Bureau and would know most things about the Security Executive.

"It could indeed but hardly immediately. Provided you don't give them concrete evidence there's very little either can do. This isn't a police state just yet, though there are people who like to pretend it is. They could call you up and give you a grilling, but I'm confident you can deal with that."

There was a time, he was thinking, when he wouldn't have said it.

Michael Henshawe thought it over silently; at last he nodded. "So for the moment you don't think that's urgent?"

"No. But something else is extremely urgent. Maoui also knew where those guns are hidden. We've got to recover them before Pallant's men get to them."

"I'll go tonight," Henshawe said at once.

"That is good – very good. You will need assistance? I have a couple of men I can trust."

"So have I. They own a furniture business and therefore a lorry. We used it to move the arms from the embassy. Equally we can use it again."

... He's much better than I thought he was.

"You can really go tonight?"

"Of course."

"And if Pallant moves first?"

"He won't move in daylight. Too many people might notice –

25

ask questions."

It was Abdel's turn to think it over. "How long to pack and move those weapons?"

"There are quite a few cases. Say a couple of hours."

"Suppose Pallant's move should clash with yours?"

"That we shall have to play by ear."

"I'm content that you do so," Abdel said. He was more content than he had dared to hope. It had been an interview against the clock but Henshawe hadn't fussed or panicked. "Keep me in touch, please." Abdel wrote down a number. "That should be safe until midday tomorrow. After that you'll have your telephone tapped and probably be tailed as well."

When Abdel had gone Henshawe rang his two friends, then cooked himself an omelette crossly. He was cross because he had wanted to rest before an outing which might well be strenuous, but Barbara had the unhappy knack of never being there when needed. He had taken her to his bed but little else, and there were moments when what he felt for her was neither affection nor even lust but a secret contempt for her half-baked commitment to causes even less baked than half. She had it all on the tip of her tongue, the fashionable sub-Marxist patter, the endless anti-American rantings. And she didn't need to be like that, she wasn't the type, she was going to be rich. There was a thriving estate on the coast in Pembrokeshire, Little England beyond Wales, but beautiful. She was an only child, she was going to inherit. She should have stayed at home and played Lady Bountiful, helping the local vicar do nothing, arranging the flowers and running the pony club. That wasn't a bad life, far from it, and there were times when Henshawe's contempt changed to envy.

And she'd thrown it all away for what? For the Foundation for the Advancement of African Rights. Like most men Henshawe believed it a front but if something more sinister stood behind it Barbara would hardly have part in that. They'd be unlikely to trust her with anything serious. Officially she was some sort of secretary but he had guessed that she offered other services. For Barbara liked men, all sorts of men, and in FAAR she would meet plenty. Men of a certain kind.

Henshawe shrugged but with a hint of distaste. Her great-grandfather had been a successful sugar planter and a psychiatrist would make much of that, nattering of the trauma of past exploitation, of the secret but driving need to atone. Which she apparently did at the drop of a hat, though that was not the first word he had thought of. Meanwhile she met his simple needs and occasionally would cook and clean.

He hadn't an idea she'd been planted.

Charles Russell was waiting quietly for Pallant when the evening newspaper came through the letterbox. He took it for the Stock Exchange prices and normally didn't bother to read it but this evening the headline screamed in outrage.

DIPLOMAT SHOT DEAD IN STREET

Russell threw the paper down in a rage . . . Another bloody Arab vendetta and in London there'd been too many already.

He was stumping the room in a bitter rage when the telephone rang. He picked it up and Pallant's voice said:

"Have you seen the paper or heard the news?" Pallant was normally quiet and collected, but this evening he was clearly upset.

"I threw it on the floor and kicked it. Childish, I know, but that's how I felt."

"There are others who will feel worse. Such as me."

"Since when have you been responsible for the chore of guarding foreign diplomats?"

"I'm not, thank God, but it isn't so simple. You know that file I sent you on Henshawe?"

"I read it with the greatest interest."

"Henshawe is connected."

"I doubt it."

"Not with the shooting. With something more serious."

"You're being tiresomely mysterious, but when you come round here –"

"I'm not coming round, or not this evening. I've got to await a certain event, or rather which way the event develops. If it goes one way it's fairly straightforward but if it were to go the other we're in the biggest mess for several years."

"It's a pity this is an open line."

27

"I'd need more than a telephone to put you in the picture properly." A pause, then: "Can you come here tomorrow?"

"If you think I could be useful."

"I do. Meeting at eleven o'clock but come at half-past ten and I'll brief you first."

"Meeting?" Russell enquired; he disliked them.

"Just the people concerned – myself and two others. James Bullen, the man I sent round, and Willy."

"William Wilberforce Smith? I look forward to seeing him."

"At half-past ten, then?"

"I'll be there."

Chapter 3

Willy Smith had seen the evening news but only with a single eye; he had been watching his wife Amanda feed the baby. Like Russell he'd thought of some Arab vendetta and was surprised when Pallant said on the telephone:

"That killing earlier this evening."

"I caught the name." He had been very carefully trained about telephones.

"Then no doubt you have made your own deductions."

"No," Willy said, "no deductions whatever."

"You surprise me but never mind. I have. I can only hope they're completely wrong but in any case I'm staying up. Instead of Harry here on radio-watch I'm going to do it myself. Good luck."

"Thank you, sir. Good night."

"You're an optimist."

Willy had only been married a year, to Amanda Dee who'd been called the Princess; he was enjoying his domesticity thoroughly and was a little resentful of interruptions. He went back to his wife a trifle huffily. The baby had had its fill and was fast asleep. "Who was that?" she asked.

"Jack Pallant. And edgy."

She was at once alert. "Some change of plan?" She knew he was going out on a night job but changes of plan were always ominous.

"No change of plan but he's steamed himself up. He's going to listen to my signals himself."

She was partly reassured and said: "So you're leaving at eleven?"

"As arranged."

"There's nothing on the box."

"There seldom is."

At eleven o'clock he went down to the street and a biggish black car slid up beside him. The driver dismounted and gave him the keys, then silently slipped away into the darkness. Willy got in and drove away.

He drove clear of London and stopped in a lay-by. Under the dashboard was a considerable radio, more than powerful enough to cover forty miles. It was his intention to check it was working properly. Radios had been known to malfunction and to arrive on station without a link would be a fiasco he didn't intend to invite. The set was both powerful and also two-way: there was no need for radio mumbo-jumbo, the 'Are you receiving me?' 'Loud and Clears' so favoured by agents on bad television. He simply pressed a button and waited. A light would be flashing on Pallant's desk.

His voice said promptly: "Willy?"

"Yes. I'm clear of London and thought I'd check."

"Everything in order this end. Call again when you start your recce."

Willy went back to his driving, satisfied. He had maps in his pocket but no need to use them. He read maps well and had done his homework, visualising this country perfectly. He took a side road and then a cart track confidently. Soon he found what he wanted, an old brick bridge. Below it was a disused canal. He hid the car in a little wood but not before calling Pallant back.

"Ready to move, sir."

"And we're ready here."

They would be, Willy thought – they had it on ice. The planning was simple and therefore good. In his pocket was a key to the pillbox and if he found guns he would radio promptly. Then the back-up party would move at once, policemen in plain clothes and with lorries. The Executive would stay where it liked to be, firmly in its own cool shadows. For the police it would be the old, old story, Acting on Information Received, and if they were lucky and reasonably quiet there might not even be need of that, just an arms haul which they needn't publicise.

Willy got down and sniffed the night like an animal. It was late autumn with its unmistakable smell but the Met men had for once been right: there wasn't any fog to obscure the moon. It rode high in the heavens as proud as a queen, but a queen who was no longer inviolate. Occasionally a small cloud hid her, then was gone and she was back in her majesty.

Willy climbed down from the bridge to the tow-path, relieved to find that it still existed. The canal had not been used for years and he knew that unused tow-paths often fell in.

He began to walk along it deliberately, almost silent in his rubber-soled shoes. He liked the night since he felt it friendly, and as he walked the map in his head came to life. This country was much as that map had told him, a tract of rather second-class farmland between two stretches of modern urban development. The canal ran down its spine, bisecting it, to the left some sadly neglected woodland, but to the right open fields and a shabby old farmhouse. A mile beyond it would be the single-line railway which slanted gently across the fields till it met the canal.

Willy had been almost silent but the geese had heard him and had started to clamour. He drooped behind a hedge at once. He grinned for he'd heard this story at Harrow. He used his night-glasses and nodded, relaxing. They came from East Germany and were the best in the world. There were geese all right but no sign of movement. Whoever lived in the farmhouse weren't Romans. He looked at it again and frowned. A pity that such a fine old building should now be falling down, uninhabited. The farmer would live elsewhere with all mod cons.

He got up again and started to walk, then froze as an animal crossed the tow-path. A tree had fallen across the canal and the badger ran across it nimbly, flat-stomached against the tree's round bole. Ten seconds later another followed it. Willy would have liked to find the set. There might be cubs and he'd never seen one.

Instead he went on steadily, counting the fields on his right as he passed them. In the fourth would be the pillbox if that ambassador had not been lying.

He had not, it was there still and Willy stared. He had heard that these futile fortifications were often somewhat eccentrically sited and this one made no military sense. The railway had come into view on the right and one of the gunslits covered the track. Against attack by an armoured train, perhaps. The other covered the old canal, presumably against invasion by sea. There was a field of fire but totally useless since behind it was a belt of scrub. A tank could hide there and shell the pillbox to rubble. Even a two-pounder would do it, for it wasn't more solid than bricks and a little cement. And any infantry worth the name would work round it, there was plentiful cover for men trained to use it. Then a grenade through one of the slits and finish.

Some respected general, long retired and half gaga, had built a deathtrap for the local home guard.

He had started to walk towards it openly when he heard movement and saw a light. He dropped. He crawled to a patch of dock which hid him but it wasn't so high that he couldn't see over it. On the opposite side of the field was a gate and a man had got down from a van to open it. The van was running without its lights and, for a moment, a wisp of cloud obscured the moon. Willy could hear that the van was moving and when the moon cleared he could see it had stopped. It had moved to the pillbox, had turned and was backing in. It was still without lights but was letting its ramp down. Three men went behind the pillbox and two came out. They were carrying a long wooden crate. They put it in the van and returned. Once, twice ...

Somewhere a dog had begun to bark furiously. Willy Smith heard a shot. The dog stopped barking.

... Well of course they'd have arms, that pillbox was stuffed with them.

He lowered his head and began to think carefully. One thing was clear: they had got there first. Whoever they were, and the worst of luck to them. They were armed which was a complication but that didn't affect the essential. Which was time. Including the walk down the disused tow-path it had taken Willy two hours to get here. The back-up party in lorries would take more. But the van was a big one, the crates looked heavy. Perhaps a handful of men in a very fast car ...

It was an outside chance but his duty to take it. Nobody but an undisciplined fool would challenge three men with weapons unarmed. He had to get back to that radio urgently and after that it was up to Pallant. He didn't have a walkie-talkie which in any case would be out of range.

He had begun to crawl backwards when he was aware of the dog. Maybe they had missed before or perhaps this was a different animal. In any case it was going to betray him. It was a country dog and was doing its duty. Here was an unexplained stranger at night . . . The dog sniffed Willy all over suspiciously, then it sat on its haunches and bayed the moon.

At once there was another shot. The dog fell over; the dog was dead. And something which Willy thought more ominous, for two more shots had whined over his head. They had missed the tops of the dock but not by much.

Again he put his head down and thought. They knew now they were being watched, and they had only to brown the patch of dock and sooner or later they'd surely get him. Or perhaps they would just walk up and risk a grenade. He shook his head for it didn't look like it.

They were pinning him to the ground by fire while they got away with those arms at their leisure. They wouldn't want to leave a body but gunfire would bring nobody running. There was a military town just a few miles distant and military noises were a part of the ambience. If anybody thought at all he would think it was some exercise by night.

Willy Smith let out a furious grunt and swore. It was humiliating, it gnawed at his liver. He'd been shot at before and hadn't enjoyed it but he hadn't been alone as a target. It had been a spraygun too but an old man behind it. The man behind that rifle wasn't old.

He shifted his position and looked again. There were only two men working now so the third would be inside with the rifle. As if to confirm his thinking there was another shot. Again it was above by inches.

He risked a roll on his shoulder to look out sideways. Forty yards to his right was a tree and a hedge, and behind them a belt of broken-down woodland. If he could reach that hedge he had a reasonable chance. They wouldn't know which way he'd gone and if it came to a chase he was fit and fleet . . . Crawl for it? No, it was much too far. He'd have to stand up and run for his life.

He hesitated but he'd made up his mind. He waited for another cloud, then began to rise to his feet.

He didn't. He wasn't even fully upright when the bullet sang viciously past his ear. He fell back into the dock and swore again.

. . . Whoever's behind that rifle is pretty damned good. He can hold me here till they've finished loading.

It took two hours with a shot at the quarters. Willy fumed but Willy knew he'd had it. They didn't want an unexplained body but they'd kill all right if he forced them to do it.

By half-past three they had filled the van. Willy could hear it drive away. He stood up cautiously and no shot came. He went back to the tow-path and walked to his car. He didn't run – there was no point in running.

Chapter 4

At half-past ten of the clock precisely Charles Russell was shown into Pallant's room. It had once been his own and he looked around curiously. Between himself and Jack Pallant had been another incumbent and he had had the tastes of his age. He had put down carpet from wall to wall and on one of them had hung an Abstract. But Pallant had exposed the fine boards again and on the walls were competent copies of Munnings. One was of a famous racehorse though Pallant wasn't a racing man, and on the opposite a Burmese girl simpered. She was pretty but unmistakably sly. There was a biggish round table with four formal chairs but for the moment they sat in leather ones comfortably.

"Nice of you to come."

"On the contrary."

"I promised you a brief and here it is." Pallant handed it over and Russell read.

When he had done so, he said uneasily, "I hope Willy Smith wasn't shot."

"He was not. It appears that they weren't shooting to kill, just to pin him down while they moved the weapons. One white man and a couple of blacks."

"And they succeeded?"

"They did."

"Then back to square one."

"Or one below it. Any questions before I call Willy and Bullen?"

Russell considered. "Just one," he said finally. "The name of the man which you say Maoui gave you."

"I sent you his file last night."

"And I've brought it back."

The words covered an almost total astonishment. Russell had read the file with sympathy, and though an embittered man was potentially dangerous it hadn't been the file of an agent. Pallant saw Russell's surprise and said:

"I read you. Henshawe isn't an operator and he hasn't been

35

trained. But if we assume as I think we must that it was he and a couple of friends last night, then he acted with commendable promptitude. He wasn't afraid to use a weapon nor so foolish as to shoot to kill. You must admit it was a high class performance."

"Very high class indeed," Russell said. He meant it. This was way above a mere bloody-mindedness.

"So now if that's all I'll call Willy and Bullen."

Pallant used a telephone and the two men came into the room together. Bullen, who'd once been a soldier, clicked. Willy Smith said politely: "Good morning, sir." Russell noticed that he was looking tired but he didn't appear in any way shaken. They all sat down at the businesslike table and Pallant asked Russell:

"Which aspect first?"

"As they happened in time – the ambassador's murder. May I ask your own interest?"

"My interest is to have none whatever, to leave it to the police entirely. I think they'll present it as I'd present it myself, as just another Arab vendetta, barbarians shooting it out in London."

"There've been more than enough to make that credible."

"But suppose the shot came from *inside* the embassy. Think of the diplomatic flap, the wholly insoluble complications. Such a thing would have to go up to the cabinet."

"And was it?" Russell asked.

"I don't know that and nor do the police. As briefed by my old friend the commissioner the bullet came from an HV weapon. It went clean through Maoui and nicked his driver."

"Awkward," Russell said.

"Extremely. For the inference would be inescapable: that while Maoui was busily grassing to me somebody else had been grassing on Maoui. So the old man sends one of his sons to London and Maoui gets shot at his own front door. If the shot did come from inside the embassy."

Russell asked quietly: "Any evidence?"

"Unhappily yes, but it isn't conclusive. A woman was walking along the street, a cleaner in another embassy, and she's been to the police and made a statement. She's said she noticed a window open and at it a man's head and shoulders ... Did she notice anything else? Well, yes. The man had seemed to be holding

36

something . . . Was it a rifle? She started to dither. First she said it *could* be a rifle, then she lost her head and withdrew what she'd said. But she stuck firmly to the head and shoulders bit."

"A coroner would tear that to pieces."

"The right sort of coroner."

"Well, who's this one?"

"He's a man who would like three letters after his name." Nobody laughed or even smiled. They were men of the world and understood perfectly.

Pallant turned to James Bullen. "You go on."

Bullen looked at a paper; he was a meticulous man. "Fortunately there is contrary evidence. There were two other men in the street at the time and one of them ran for his life when the shot was fired. The other says he was some sort of Asian. Whether it was he or not it's certain we'll never see him again. The one thing an Asian won't do is help the police."

"The suggestion will be it was he killed Maoui?"

"If it's properly handled."

"I'm sure it will be. But what about the HV bullet?"

"Several modern hand-guns have that sort of kick."

"And the driver?"

"Will presumably say what Abdel tells him to."

Russell had sat up sharply. "Abdel?"

"Abdelaziz on more formal occasions."

"Is he the old man's son, the new counsellor?"

"That's the man. But of course we're still guessing."

Russell opened his mouth to speak but shut it. He had met Abdelaziz once before but this wasn't the moment for ancient tales. He nodded and said: "Thank you. I see."

Jack Pallant had come in again. "So that's the police side – I wish them luck."

"Do you think they'll get away with it?"

"Just. Now let's move to what *is* my interest – those weapons."

"Which returns us to Michael Henshawe." Russell frowned. "One thing I would bet much money on. They're not destined for the I.R.A. who have sources of their own already."

"I never supposed they were."

"Then for whom?"

Pallant said to Bullen: "Yours again." Bullen drew a long breath.

"The blacks."

William Wilberforce Smith didn't move an eyebrow. He thought of himself as a coloured Englishman and provided you didn't use words like nigger he didn't give a damn how you put it.

Russell wondered how Bullen was going to handle it for this was very sensitive ground. You mustn't say 'ghetto' but 'concentration' or 'enclave' since the whole subject was wrapped in political flannel. There'd been a race riot in Bristol and what had happened? Within hours a senior politician had gone on the box to insist that it hadn't been. Charles Russell couldn't remember his reasoning for he had spoken much too fast and too fluently. Russell had switched him off and laughed, and in a million homes across the country there'd been the same quick clicks and the same sour laughter. The politician had not heard either and wouldn't have minded if somehow he had. He was a notably self-important man.

Charles Russell grimaced for he could recognise folly. In the Japanese empire before the war there'd been a crime called Harbouring Dangerous Thoughts. It hadn't come quite to that in Britain, they couldn't pull you in and torture you, but if you made the least slip they would pounce at once, the protectors of orthodox thinking on colour. They had even changed the law against you. They didn't, now, have to prove intention, only that offence had been given. Charles Russell was civilised and therefore tolerant and this was a sort of intolerance in reverse. Euphoric pretence had taken over from policy.

But Bullen had passed him a newspaper cutting. "That puts it a great deal better than I could." It was a piece about a chief constable under the headline, 'Black Mischief'.

Last week he levelled a very serious charge against Britain's 'race relations industry': that it has been infiltrated by agitators whose express purpose is to increase tension rather than decrease it. Hitherto most of us have assumed that when these race organisations made matters worse it was through folly and ignorance rather than ill-will. Not so, says the chief constable.

Conscious subversion also plays its baleful part.

Race relations obviously do offer politically-motivated subversives ample opportunity for subversion, and the chief constable has already produced some evidence. The Home Office has a duty to look into the matter and to let the people know what is going on.

"Small hope of that," Charles Russell said. "Far too many men and women make comfortable livings in race relations. But apart from this brave and conscientious chief constable, what do you know yourselves?"

"Very little." It was Pallant again and Pallant was frowning. "We know there are cells in the major ghettos. 'Cells' isn't a word I use too happily but for the moment there isn't another that fits." He began to reel off an alarming list. "But at that point we get hamstrung by our skins. It's an obvious case for infiltration but black policemen are few and far between and in any case are immediately spotted."

Russell found he was looking at Willy but dropped his eyes. Willy would make a very poor infiltrator. He spoke without a trace of accent and he dressed very carefully, even fastidiously. He favoured a bowler hat at all times and sometimes he carried a rolled umbrella. He looked like a well-connected executive leaving a merchant bank at half-past five.

"Do you know who fronts for these cells?"

"Not yet."

"It could be any of several similar set-ups. FAAR, for instance."

"Why them?"

"It's on Henshawe's file that he lives with a girl in it."

"Not enough," Pallant said at once. "By a mile."

"But a possible lead." Charles Russell considered, then said reluctantly: "So we're facing a very disturbing set-up. Here are cells on the one side and arms on the other – arms floating around the country at large and with no sort of clue where to start a search. If the two get married you wouldn't like it."

"Something of an understatement. Bristol was contained in the end but there weren't any guns to make it bloodier. In Florida they had arms and used them. And we do not have a national guard. It would have to be the army or nothing and that could bring any government crashing."

"How do you think they'd use guns if they had them?"

"You want my private opinion?"

"Yes, of course."

"They might not turn them on us to start with, they might turn them on the Indians first. You know what a black man thinks about Indians and you know what happened to them in Africa. It was economic folly no doubt, but I think I understand the motives."

"The Indians or ourselves it would come to the same. I believe we recently formed a riot squad though in the present climate we don't dare call it one. But it isn't very big."

"It is not," Pallant said.

"Then back to the army."

"With rubber bullets."

"You've got to be speaking in jest."

"I was. A poor one. Rubber bullets don't go far against real ones."

"So bloody fighting in several major cities. So down with any conceivable government which happens to be muddling along."

"I said that myself."

"And I didn't dissent." Charles Russell looked at Pallant hard. "What are you going to do?" It was brutal.

"I was going to ask your advice, sir." It was cool.

"You could have Henshawe up and play him by ear."

"On his form last night I doubt if he'd scare."

"I wasn't suggesting you try to scare him. I wasn't even suggesting you see him yourself."

"Then who?"

"Who but Willy."

"Willy?"

"You heard me. Try to see it from Henshawe's side of the fence. If he's thinking of giving those guns to blacks there's no possible harm in a visible lesson that there are other sorts of blacks than potential rioters. There might even be some small advantage, though I wouldn't lean too hard on that."

He was also thinking but did not say that both men came from the

40

same social class. But 'class' was a word like 'ghetto' or 'negro' which nowadays one uttered with diffidence. There were people who would flinch if they heard them. Charles Russell thought it unrealistic to throw away good words without reason. They had been succeeded by half-breeds like 'underprivileged' on the one hand, and on the other the equally shameful 'elitist'. But there was no profit in an unnecessary risk. He held his peace.

Pallant said to Willy: 'Can do?'

"I can have a try but suppose he won't come?"

Charles Russell said: "Then you'll have to persuade him."

"How?" It was Pallant. "I daren't use the rough stuff. Not if he's got the connections we suspect."

"I wasn't suggesting the rough stuff."

"Then what?"

"Do you still employ Anne Bullen?"

"She's still on call."

Anne Bullen was James Bullen's sister and a lady of some worldly experience. She carried neither cosh nor gun but could charm the birds from the trees and sometimes did.

Pallant turned to Bullen. "All right by you?"

"It's entirely up to her, sir."

"Right. I'll get in touch at once. Where is she?"

"In London."

"Not at that broken-down castle of yours?" It was very small but still a castle.

James Bullen didn't appear offended. "The broken-down castle is uninhabited except for an incompetent caretaker. We've been trying to sell it for years but no one will buy."

"No one, if I may say so, is right."

"And the National Trust says it's gone too far."

"A pity, that." Pallant hated waste; he turned to Russell. "I'll put a first-class man on Henshawe but I doubt if he'll give much away. Is there anything else?"

"Nor for my part. Nothing."

The four men rose and Pallant showed Charles Russell to the front door. The action was one of respect, not necessity, since Russell knew the geography perfectly. He went back to the others to tidy the ends up, handing Henshawe's file to Willy.

41

"Willy, go and do your homework before you think of talking to Henshawe. You'll find that file is mainly background – potential trouble, not anything concrete – but in the last few hours it has changed its nature. James, I'd like a word alone."

Willy went out and Pallant waved at a chair. James Bullen sat down in it, apprehensive. To send Willy out was most unusual.

Pallant was more than apprehensive, Jack Pallant was an embarrassed man. He had something to say of the greatest delicacy and he wasn't very good at nuances. He would have preferred to say nothing but felt he must speak. Since he knew he wasn't very good at the soft stuff he went at it straight to get it over.

"There was mention of FAAR, as you heard. Also of a Barbara Rhys-Harte."

Bullen was silent since he'd guessed what was coming. If he hadn't dropped Barbara Rhys-Harte they'd have fired him. And perfectly correctly too. An officer of the Executive must be seen to be Caesar's wife and remain so, but in fact he had broken it off quite voluntarily. Not that there had been any engagement, simply, on his part, a strong attraction till he'd discovered what sort of woman she was . . . All that fashionable patter about race relations, the job in that absurd Foundation! You could live with that on the basis of shack-up and a man called Henshawe apparently did so, but as a basis for life for forty years it hadn't borne consideration.

And now Pallant was breathing the ashes to life again, and he wasn't being mealy-mouthed. He was asking:

"Do you see her still?"

"I see her at occasional parties where I light her cigarette and bring her a drink."

"You must forgive me, if you can, for pressing you. There's been nothing else?"

"Nothing whatever."

"No telephone calls?"

"I have never rung her. If she has rung me I have not received it."

Jack Pallant said: "I'm delighted to hear it."

If that was an apology it was something less than handsome.

James Bullen went back to his room and frowned. It struck him as grossly unfair, a meanness. He hadn't been prised away from

Barbara, he had seen that she was a hollow woman. And now he knew what had happened precisely. Somewhere, like every other employee, he'd have a secret and very personal file and on that file was a very bad mark. Indelible, inexpungeable, permanent. He had never been trained as an outside operator, and though in his heart he resented this his intelligence told him it was probably just. He simply didn't have those talents. But to be marked down for what he hadn't done, endangering the Executive's security . . .

One day, he thought, I'll get rid of that blot. I'll pull some great coup and show them. I will.

Unknowingly he had spoken aloud but he knew as he heard the words they were false. He would pull no great coup since they wouldn't let him. They would offer not even the sniff of a chance at it.

Russell's normal pre-luncheon drink was sherry but this morning he felt he had earned something stronger. He poured a gin and Angostura bitters and sat down with it to consider the morning.

He decided it hadn't gone too ill. At least they had faced the facts about those arms, the admission that they were floating freely, the acceptance that a search for them would be useless without some clue to start from. There were countries where this would be perfectly simple: you would pull in Henshawe and beat it out of him, but all you could do in England was to ask him to call. If he chose not to come you must think again, and Russell felt he'd been useful there. It was a question of knowing your man and he'd read Henshawe's file. Whatever the man was he wasn't a coward. Send a strongarm round and he wouldn't budge, and if the strongarm tried tricks Michael Henshawe might match them. But send him a mature, worldly woman and he would probably come out of mere politeness.

So the idea to use Anne Bullen had been sound, and there was a second matter he was entitled to feel pleased about. For though he'd admitted that he'd met Abdelaziz he hadn't bored them with a wartime story or told them that every Christmas Abdel sent him a card. It was written in calligraphic Arabic which Russell couldn't begin to read but at the end was an unvarying message in an English of extreme simplicity. It said: 'I thank you again,' and left it at that.

Normally Russell drank wine with his luncheon but this morning he knew there was going to be curry, and with that there could only be water or lager. He would allow himself another stiff gin.

Over it his good humour faded since the meeting had left one subject wide open. Those cells, he thought – they had sounded ominous. They would need a front and he had asked who was raising it, but the real question was not who fronted but who controlled. The easy answer was Michael Henshawe, the man who had the means to arm them, but the easy answer was mostly wrong. Charles Russell had a long experience and he permitted himself a decided scepticism ... A white man touring the major ghettos, organising groups of blacks? Unlimited money would buy adherents but would they be the men you wanted? Whereas a dedicated black could do it. He, Russell, had properly spoken of cover: the cells would have some innocuous title like Committees for Mutual Aid and Protection, and a formal and quite open connection with maybe FAAR or something like it. But *control* of them, control of their purpose was something which was so far hidden. It was useless to speculate Who? without a lead.

And that admirable chief constable had said nothing about the cells having arms. If they had he would have surely said so since it would have strengthened his hand by the ace of trumps. So it was safe to assume that they hadn't – yet. But Michael Henshawe had weapons ...

Charles Russell ate, then burped uninhibitedly. There were civilisations where not to do so was considered really shocking manners. He sat in his chair content in body but in his mind there was an increasingly nagging worry. If there was really a Big Boy behind those cells, if he didn't have weapons whilst Henshawe had ...

Then before there was any organised rioting there was going to be a private war.

William Wilberforce Smith went home at six to the ugly old house near Clapham Common. Willy was third-generation British and his father had made a considerable fortune. He could well have

44

afforded to move somewhere smarter but he'd been born in that house in a two-room flat and there he'd intended to die owning all of it. Six months ago he had done so peacefully, leaving Willy very comfortably off. The house was now two maisonettes. In the top one lived Willy's widowed mother with a companion who was unashamedly white, but the two old ladies had both been nurses and knew each other's habits perfectly. In the bottom maisonette lived Willy with Amanda Dee whom he'd married a year ago. He thought of her as he walked from the station. She was fourth generation which put her one up and her father, too, had been passing rich, but Willy hadn't married for money, admirable as the match had been. He had married because he had liked and admired her. He thought her a very smart girl indeed, and in a single year she had twice seen clearly when he himself had been fumbling blindly. Maybe she wasn't a raving beauty but she had loved him and was an excellent wife. A man who married for lust was an ass, particularly in the establishment classes like Willy.

Amanda said as he hung up his hat: "You're looking pretty knackered."

"I am a bit. I didn't get a lot of sleep."

"Nor did I but for rather different reasons. Thank you for not waking me when I'd dropped off."

He knew that she lost sleep with the baby and had gone to the spare room as a matter of course. The bed had been made and the sheets were aired. Amanda was an excellent housekeeper.

She naturally knew where he worked and at what, indeed her own father had greatly approved of it, but she also understood that he couldn't talk. So she didn't ask where he'd been last night but simply said:

"You were terribly late."

"It got a bit hairy."

"Take care."

"Oh, I do."

They were eating chicken, fried bananas and sweetcorn. Amanda, like Willy, had been expensively educated but her mother had taught her to cook and well. At the end Willy said:

"That was quite delicious."

"The bird? I got it in the Market, you know."

45

"Most of the stuff there has fallen off the back of a lorry."

"But since you're not a policeman, why worry?"

There was a famous Market two miles south-east of them. The whole area had a geographical name, an Underground station, a London postcode. But it was never called anything else but 'the Market'.

"I'm not worried about who pilfers what and from where. I'm worried about your still using the Market."

She looked at him thoughtfully. "I realise it's changed."

"It used to be jolly and very much ours. The only rule was mind your own business. Perhaps it's the Indians – they've begun to move in – and you know what we feel about Indian traders. If anything rubs us up raw it's them."

"I'm not a Wog and I doubt if it's that. I've never had even a dirty look, just chaff about talking posh and buying the best. I've had to take those jokes for quite a time. Once it annoyed me but now it doesn't."

"Is that all you have to tell me?"

"What? I thought it was you telling me."

"It was. Now I'm asking you."

"Try to make a bit more sense, dear."

"You're a very smart girl and you keep your eyes open."

She considered again. "The change in atmosphere? It's nothing really."

"Nothing can be an awful lot."

"I sometimes get a sort of, well *smell*. That something's brewing below the surface. There are still lots of jokes and plenty of smiles – at some stalls, that is, but not at all."

"And where there are neither jokes nor smiles?"

"I can only call it a sort of tension."

"Anything to put behind that?"

"Twice I've heard men talk of the Saviours."

"Were they Rastas?"

"No, they were short-back-and-siders."

He said a little disapprovingly: "Some of us are very religious. We run from Popery right down the ladder, down to rolling on the floor and screaming." He himself was cosily Anglican. His mentors had been too civilised to demand that he believe but they had insisted that he conform and he still did.

"I don't think they meant that sort of Saviour."

If he asked her why he would sound a fool. She could see further through a brick wall than he could. "Are you sure you're safe?"

"As safe as in Bond Street, maybe safer. A man tried to snatch my bag once. He was white."

"What happened then?"

"A black knocked him down and gave me the bag back. The white ran away and that was that. I gave the black a fiver. He thanked me."

"Take care of yourself," Willy Smith said uneasily.

"I said that to you last night and what happened?"

"I slept in the spare bed," he said, "but I don't propose to do that tonight."

Chapter 5

Abdelaziz had given Henshawe a number and Henshawe had duti-
fully rung him back the morning after his brush with Willy. He'd
said: "Successful but a complication."

"Was there indeed? We must speak about that."

And a great many other things, Abdel was thinking. Their last
talk had been a talk under pressure, the need for some immediate
action, but now he had several questions to ask, the most
important of which was how far Henshawe had moved towards
forming any organisation. It didn't advance his father's plan,
which he still privately thought of as overreaction, to bring in guns
and successfully hide them if there weren't the men to use them
effectively. Abdel asked:

"Can we meet this morning? Say at eleven?"

"I can make an excuse to get away from the paper." An excuse
about the Market perhaps. There was often some sort of story
there – not a big one yet, but the pot was boiling. "Are you coming
to my flat?"

"Not this time. You'll be shadowed by now and very possibly
bugged. Do you know a suitable public house?"

"The Goat and Compasses. It's in a pretty quiet street."
Michael Henshawe named it.

"Very well. At eleven."

Abdel would have preferred it earlier but he had made another
appointment at half-past nine. It was one with the police who had
telephoned courteously and he didn't think it wise to put them off.

The chief inspector was punctual and wore a well-tailored
uniform. He saluted before he was asked to sit down and then
opened the game with a careful cliché.

"It is kind of you to see me, sir. You must be a very busy man."

"Certainly the ambassador's murder has meant a lot of extra
work."

"To which I am very sorry to add. But there are one or two loose
ends to tidy."

49

"If I can help you in any way I will."

The gambits had been made and properly met. Now for the game, the inspector thought. A good deal was going to depend on its outcome. "Apart from the chauffeur two people were in the street at the time and the stories they tell are inconsistent. One was a man and the other a woman. The man heard a shot, saw an Asian running. He is unshakable that the man was an Asian. Would you care to comment on that?"

"You mean if the man had been an Arab you would have accepted it a lot more easily? I take the point and offer apologies. There *have* been countries, though not my own, which have disgraced themselves by shoot-ups in London."

"But given that the man *was* an Asian?"

"You are wondering what Asian could wish for revenge?" Abdelaziz considered carefully. This story of an Asian gunman was a large slice of luck and quite uncovenanted. He did not wish to throw it away. Finally he said: "None or any. In my country there were not very many but what there were we did get rid of, and perhaps one or two of them came to England. Would you care for me to see if we've records?"

"I don't think we need trouble you, sir."

It had been uttered as though on a practised cue and Abdel looked at the policeman shrewdly. He's had his instructions, he thought, and he'll stick to them. That Asian who panicked and took to his heels was a stroke of good fortune for me and mine but it was also a stroke of good luck for the police. He'll never be heard of again and that is that. Whereas an Asian who'd been expelled from my country and was later found to be here in England . . . There'd have to be an organised drag and an organised drag for a refugee. The police wouldn't want that and their masters would loathe it. It was one thing for alien Arabs to break the rules, quite another for some coloured immigrant to be hunted down for a political crime. Every bleeding heart in the country would squeal with pain. So the police had decided to fudge it. Good.

The inspector's next words confirmed this obliquely. "We didn't really expect you to help us."

"I'm sorry," Abdel said. It wasn't true.

The inspector drew a careful breath; he was coming to the

50

difficult part but he'd been well rehearsed and knew his lines.

"Then on the other hand we have this woman. She's a cleaner in another embassy and was on the other side of the road to the shooting. She heard a shot and looked up at your embassy. Her story is more than a little confused and in fact she has changed it when questioned thoroughly. But in essence she saw a window open and at it a man's head and shoulders. She also had a vague impression, and I must emphasise the adjective strongly, that the man was holding some sort of weapon."

As indeed I was, Abdelaziz thought.

He hadn't a doubt that the police suspected him but he doubted if they would wish to pursue it. An unknown Asian was an easier let-out than pursuing an accredited diplomat. Any sane policeman would shrink from that and those above wouldn't urge him to meddle. But Abdel had to be sure and he started to probe.

"Men go to windows for many reasons. They may, for instance, feel a need for some air."

"I entirely agree," the inspector said. It came pat again, another on cue.

. . . He's had his instructions, they're going to smother it. I can risk a direct question and I will.

"What sort of woman was she?"

"Uneducated."

"Would she make a good witness?"

"They would rip her to pieces."

"Then one last question, please."

"By all means."

"His excellency's driver, then?"

"Was, as you know, very slightly wounded, but in hospital he made a statement." (After you'd been to see him, the policeman thought). "He confirms that he saw an Asian who ran away."

Abdel reflected; he could leave it at that. And so could the police: they intended to do so. He said as he rose:

"Again, if I can help . . ."

For the first time the inspector smiled. "You have," he said. "You have indeed." He rose in turn, saluted and took his leave. He had earned an excellent mark and would get it.

Abdel sent for a taxi and gave the address of Henshawe's pub.

51

He didn't suppose he himself would be followed but in the Bureau he had come up from near bottom and he looked through the taxi's back window with interest. Whether or not you were being followed was very largely a matter of instinct unless the follower was untrained or clumsy, so any of half a dozen vehicles might contain an efficient security tail. His instinct now was that none of them did but when he paid off the taxi he waited outside. No one came into the street but a woman. He looked at her – she was black and elderly.

He was satisfied but he waited on, tasting the street's peculiar flavour. It was one of paired mid-Victorian villas, rather prettily stuccoed and once desirable, the homes of managing clerks and shopkeepers, of young doctors starting in private practice. Now the tides of immigration had lapped it but they hadn't entirely destroyed its ambience. A sociologist . . .

He frowned as the word formed itself for it was one which he despised as meaningless, but a man interested in social history would find this street a fruitful study. One or two of these houses were singles still – one even had a magnolia tree and window boxes at all four windows where the last of the summer's annuals were withering – but mostly they were now two flats. The standard of maintenance varied wildly. Some of these villas were still well-kept, the stucco repaired in the broken patches, but others were very near to ruin and one or two were boarded up. Opposite a taxi-driver was washing a cab which matched his complexion, and the street was crammed with private cars. Mostly they were ageing jalopies but they were surprisingly big ("Well, they breed large families,") and some had been lovingly amateur-painted in colours which made Abdel blink. He checked again that he wasn't tailed, then went into the Goat and Compasses.

Henshawe was drinking a glass of lager, and as he rose he asked: "I assume you don't drink?"

"You assume entirely wrong, my friend. What is forbidden me is the juice of the grape and beer is made from yeast and hops. Any later interpretation of holy writ is a puritanical gloss".

Henshawe hid a smile as he ordered the beer. He had never practised the faith he professed but it had taught him the art of finding good reasons for doing what you intended anyway.

Abdel looked round the pub with interest. The drinkers were both white and coloured. All were respectable and they all seemed to know each other. Henshawe had chosen a separate table and Abdel looked hard at the men at the bar.

"Are you conscious of being followed?"

"No."

"I can assure you you are. It's the man in the cap. Pretty good to have got him on so quickly."

"How do you know?"

"I have a certain experience."

"I beg your pardon."

"Not at all."

"Anyway he's too far to hear us."

Abdelaziz laughed. "But is he? If you look you'll see he's wearing a hearing aid but it isn't a common-or-garden hearing aid. It's directional and extremely sensitive, and if you look again you'll see something else. He has slightly turned his stool to get us in line."

"I can see why you're the head of the Bureau. Shall we go somewhere else?"

"He or another would simply follow us."

"Then what are we going to do?"

"I'll show you. Electronics have gone some way since I was a boy." Abdel laid on the table a gold cigarette case. An arrow was faintly etched on the lid and he moved it till at last he seemed satisfied. Then he squeezed the cigarette case gently.

The man at the bar gave a scream of pain. He pulled out his aid as he fell off his stool. He held a hand to his ear and he ran from the room.

Abdel was explaining casually. "The wonders of modern science," he said. He had pocketed the cigarette case. "You've heard of those rather chi-chi dog whistles – the sort the dog can hear and you can not? Well, if you're wearing *that* sort of hearing aid the spectrum of your hearing is much increased. What I sent him was a very loud noise. I hope I didn't burst his ear drum. The poor donkey was only doing his duty."

The beer had come to their table and Abdel drank some. "Thank you for your earlier message. I gather you have the weapons."

"I have."

"That is very well done. Congratulations. But you also spoke of complications."

"Pallant's men got there too."

"Why Pallant's?"

"Because the late unlamented Maoui told Pallant where the stuff was hidden. As far as we know he told nobody else."

Abdelaziz nodded, satisfied. It struck him as entirely logical. He was also impressed and said respectfully:

"And you got it away from under their noses?"

"*His* nose – I'm sure there was only one. Pallant wouldn't want to look a fool and Maoui, for some reason unknown, could have been trying to embroil him in some political fracas. So he'd send a scout first and if arms were there –"

"I see," Abdel said. Again it was logical. "Tell me what happened," he added.

"Of course. We've assumed that Maoui told Pallant my name, but that isn't the same thing as knowing that it was I went back to the pillbox and grabbed the guns. There was a moon and the three of us weren't wearing masks. Quite apart from possible inter-ference I had to prevent that scout from getting too close. Close enough for recognition or more likely just a good description."

"Good thinking," Abdel said. "And then?"

"I had to shoot."

"So where's the body?" Abdel didn't sound surprised, only curious.

"There isn't any body."

"Kindly repeat."

"It was enough to pin him down by fire. There was a rifle with a nightsight. I used it whilst the other two loaded the van."

Abdel didn't often smile but now his craggy mountain-man's face split in an unexpected grin. A fine shot himself he respected another. "You must be very good with a rifle."

"Pretty fair. It was the only thing I did well at Sandhurst. I even got a prize for it but that didn't stop them kicking me out."

Abdelaziz accepted another beer. Like Pallant he had a file on Henshawe, since he wouldn't have employed him blind, and the affair at Sandhurst had always puzzled him. Here was officer

54

material, a first-class marksman, and they'd thrown him out for being clumsy at drill. (Except, he remembered, they wouldn't say 'clumsy'. The accepted word was always 'idle'.) And what did drill count for? In Abdel's view little. A cadet who joined the Light Division spent six months at least, and sometimes more, in learning one entirely different. Yet the fetish was enshrined for ever. That was their business but also foolish. It wasn't sensible to turn this man, potentially a faithful servant, into what he was now, an embittered enemy, an enemy serving an old man's vendetta.

And serving it, so far, surprisingly competently.

Abdel hesitated before his next question for his conscience wasn't entirely clear. The obvious place to re-hide those weapons had been his own embassy here in London, but it was one thing to smuggle in arms in the Bag, slipping them out in dribs and drabs to the man who was finally going to use them, quite another to cache a considerable armoury in an embassy already suspect. He had shied at that and had left it to Henshawe. So he asked with a certain diffidence:

"Where are the weapons now?"

"In a house in this street."

"I don't believe it."

"It's safer than it sounds, you know, and come to that what place *is* safe if the Executive mounts a full-scale hunt? The house belongs to a man of mine, one of the two I took to that pillbox. He lives alone and likes it that way – locally he's considered eccentric. So he has boarded up the top flat of his house and it's been like that for years unsuspiciously. The old widow who lives next door is deaf as a stone. That's how we slipped in the stuff at night."

Abdel wasn't entirely satisfied but he knew that he'd have to accept. "Very well. But don't go near that house yourself."

"I wasn't going to anyway, and especially not now when I know I'm shadowed. But another thing does bother me."

"Yes?"

"You suggested last time that Pallant might call me up."

"And has he?"

"Not yet."

"Let me know if he does."

"Of course I will. Do you think I should take a lawyer?"

"No. The Executive can't arrest or charge you, though if you make a slip they may possibly kill you." It was said without the least sign of emotion. Abdel was in the business too. "A lawyer wouldn't help at all."

"Then I'd better not make a slip."

"Good luck."

Abdel hesitated for he had one more question, the most awkward, as it happened, of all. Those arms were for the moment safe, though not to his mind entirely secure. But the men who were going to use them?

He didn't know.

He would have to serve his father usefully so he put his question and watched Michael Henshawe. "And how's the second side — not the weapons but their intended users?"

Henshawe had known that the question must come and had decided that half a truth would be fatal. "Not good," he said.

Again Abdelaziz showed no surprise, saying on almost a note of sympathy: "Your colour must be a disadvantage."

If this was offered as an easy way out Henshawe was too shrewd to take it. "Up to a point but beyond that it shouldn't be. There's a background of very real discontent and you'd have to be a fool not to feel it. Some of them don't do badly at all — the established old hands on the railways, for instance — but it's hard to find a job if you lose one and many young men don't have jobs to lose. They're receptive to any idea of violence, and Bristol showed what can happen when they explode. No, I can't say it's hard to get them to listen."

"Then what goes wrong?"

"It's difficult to pin it down. Besides this piece of London we're sitting in I've been to Birmingham and Cardiff and up to Glasgow, and in all of them I thought I'd made progress. Real progress, not just talk and your money. I'd met the sort who'd use arms if they had them. And then, within a week, it just melted away. I couldn't find my previous contacts and when I did they wouldn't speak to me."

"You felt there had been some counter-action? That the police or, more likely, something more secret had somehow scared your groups or broken them up?"

56

"Not quite that."

"Then what?"

"Not counter-action but competition. From somebody bigger they trusted more."

"Have you any idea who he is?"

"None at all."

Abdelaziz thought this over. It seemed to him entirely possible. The ghettos in half a dozen cities were ready to boil over in violence: it would be strange if no one had come before Henshawe. He thought, as Charles Russell had thought before him, that if this other man had effective cells whilst Henshawe had the hardware hidden ...

He was bound to his father by total loyalty but it had never been his father's intention to arm somebody else's private army.

He rose at last and for once prevaricated. "I'll be staying in London, at least for the present. Keep me in touch with any developments." But there was something else he must know before judgment and on that he must form his own opinion. "Isn't there a big market near here? I mean one which is almost entirely black?"

"The whole area is called the Market, but if you want the market itself turn right when you leave this pub. In the main street turn right again to the station. Behind it are the shops and the stalls." Henshawe looked at his watch. "It will still be crowded. I think you'll find it more than interesting."

I shall, Abdel thought – I shall indeed. There is something I must be sure of and quickly and I'll have to trust to my native senses.

In the street outside the pub he looked round again. He was confident that he wasn't shadowed himself and the street had begun to fill with people, men and women who happened to work nearby returning to their homes for their lunches. The already crowded cars were more so and there was a good deal of casual friendly joshing about who had the right to park where and for how long. Whites, he knew, would have been much less good-tempered.

He walked to the Market thinking hard, past the fine old church which still stood proudly. Henshawe had spoken of real discontent. Of course there was real discontent and resentment, some of it probably quite ill-founded and some of it entirely justified. And Henshawe had said another thing, that Bristol had shown what could happen when they exploded. Of course again – they were a volatile race. But to make any sense of his father's plan Abdel had to know one thing which he didn't. Give these men arms and would they *use* them? Perhaps they would shoot but when the bullets came back at them . . .

He was prepared to trust his own impression since this wasn't the sort of knowledge you got from a book.

So he went into the Market to observe. It was a fine autumn morning, the place was teeming. Eight out of ten were clearly West Indian but there were one or two Nigerians too, stalking past in their barbaric colours, adding a dress-rehearsal dimension to the shouting and good-humoured banter. Occasionally there was a single Indian, walking with a certain diffidence. His own stamping grounds were two miles north and he knew that he was loathed and despised. A uniformed policeman was patrolling pontifically. Nobody paid him the slightest attention. His business was not to spy on the stall-holders who, he knew perfectly well, sold stolen goods; his business was to keep the peace which in this case meant gentle intervention in some quarrel between a couple of women who happened to want the same piece of merchandise. There was little sign of poverty here. Two housewives were even sharing a taxi, loading it with the weekly shopping. It was a great deal cheaper than keeping a car and they had saved themselves money by using the market. Moreover they had clearly enjoyed it, digging each other's ribs and joking.

If I had to find a word, Abdel thought, gusto would do as well as any. That was the pulse of this place, not violence.

He didn't smoke often but now felt the need to, going into a little shop. The woman said: "Good morning, sir," and he ordered his favourite brand and matches. She had magnificent teeth and a splendid bosom and was prepared to use both to their best advantage. She had been puzzled by Abdel whom she couldn't quite place. Clearly he wasn't a black like herself, but neither was he quite her idea of a white. Finally she decided to risk it.

"I could let you have a thousand. Cheap." She named a price which made him blink.

"It would take me a year to get through a thousand."

The answer seemed to surprise and alarm her. He read her thought and said at once:

"It's perfectly true. I smoke six a day."

Her self-confidence returned with his smile. "I thought perhaps you might be a copper."

"One thing I am not is a copper. Particularly an English copper."

"You speak very good English."

"They sent me to school here."

She was more than ready to chat all the morning but he didn't believe she'd have much to tell him. If there were undercurrents in this placid stream she wasn't the sort to know they existed. "Good morning, madam."

"Good morning. Come again."

Abdel didn't eat breakfast and had begun to feel hungry. There was a café selling chicken and chips but it didn't look overclean and was crowded. He walked round a corner and found a restaurant. Rather to his surprise it was Indian, but where there was money an Indian would follow it. Fearfully perhaps, but he'd follow it. Abdel went in and sat down. He was alone.

The proprietor came up and asked him his pleasure. Abdel could tell from the way he spoke English that he was an Indian expelled from East Africa. Native-born Indians learnt their English from others, and even when they spoke it fluently they never quite lost a tell-tale cadence. But an Indian born in an East African state learnt his English from an English teacher. Like the woman in the tobacconist the proprietor couldn't quite place Abdel but he had the air of a man who could pay for a meal. He was naturally obsequious and now he almost broke his back, producing a menu with an overdone flourish.

Abdelaziz waved it aside. "Chicken curry," he said, "with saffron rice." Like Charles Russell he was fond of curry but it had to be a very good one. "And have you any ladies' fingers?"

"Alas, your honour, they are not obtainable."

"Then an aubergine, in halves, and served separately."

"Certainly, sir."

"And I'll have some chapatis."

The Indian looked doubtful. "You mean popadums, sir?"

"I do not mean popadums. Popadums are for fat Madrassis. I mean proper chapatis made with millet."

"They will take a little time, sir."

"I can wait. And please bring me a lager to pass the time."

He was glad of a moment to clear his mind for he had realised he must make a decision. He had been sent to further his father's plan and whilst that plan had a chance of success he'd be dishonoured if he failed to do so. But had it in fact any chance of success? Miami had been more than a riot, Miami had been a bloody battle, and half a dozen such around this country would have results which only a seer could foretell. That had always been his father's premise, correct but was it also practical? Henshawe had been far from successful in setting up cells to use the arms, and more important, as he'd seen it this morning, these people were not American Negroes with a history of political strife.

He sat and sipped his beer, undecided. From the kitchen came an altercation, the proprietor's voice and the voice of a woman. He guessed that the language was Gujarati.

Three young blacks had come in and sat down facing him. They were a good deal better dressed than the average and had an air which escaped exact definition. But Abdel had a long experience and he could place these three without a difficulty. They weren't yobbos, they were professional hard men.

... Curious.

The Indian went up to their table and bowed. They didn't even wish him Good Morning. The tallest took the menu and glanced at it. "I'll take the forty-four," he said.

"So will we."

"And bring us some beer."

This time the Indian looked more than doubtful.

"You heard me. Beer."

The proprietor returned to his kitchen. As he passed him Abdel could see he was trembling.

The three had ordered a standard dish and it arrived at their table while Abdel still waited. They nodded at the Indian coolly.

"Good appetite, gentlemen."

They all three laughed.

Abdelaziz watched them eat with interest – you could tell a great deal from the way a man ate. These three ate tidily, quickly and with a good enough appetite, but it was evident that none was starving. When they had finished all three stood up.

The Indian was at their table in a flash; he put the bill on it and stood there waiting, his physical fear at once submerged by the greater fear of losing money. He was smiling but the smile was sickly. The tallest man picked the bill up and tore it in four. He threw the pieces in the Indian's face.

There was shrill and instant lamentation. A low-caste Indian in obvious fear wasn't Abdelaziz's favourite object and for a moment he looked away in embarrassment. When he looked back the proprietor was weeping. He heard the word 'police' and a contemptuous laugh again.

The tall man struck like an angered snake. He feinted at the Indian's testicles, then, as he dropped his hands, chopped back-handed. The Indian went down in a tangle on the floor.

The tall man looked at the others who nodded. One of them went to the windows and drew the blinds, the other carefully locked the door. Then they began to wreck the restaurant. They did it systematically, starting on the tables and glasses, passing to the chairs and lights. When they had finished the place was a ruin. They worked in silence without a smile. One went into the kitchen. A woman screamed. When he returned all three kicked the Indian. They were kicking to injure but not to kill. When he stopped groaning they looked around, satisfied. One of them unlocked the door and they slipped into the street one by one.

Professional, Abdel thought – very expert.

None of them had even glanced at him and he hadn't felt it his business to intervene. They were three to one and younger than he was, and though he was armed and would have used it defensively the last thing he wanted was starting a shoot-up. Besides, he didn't hold Indians highly.

Nevertheless he went to the kitchen. A woman had collapsed in a chair but he could see that, though shocked, she hadn't been mauled. He went back into the restaurant coolly, thinking as he'd

61

trained to think, thinking of the practical details. He hadn't touched his cutlery but he wiped it with his handkerchief carefully. He took out a fiver and wiped that too. After all he had ordered, the food would waste. Still using his handkerchief he opened the door. The blinds were down, the place looked closed.

He slipped away and walked a mile. He then took a taxi back to his embassy. He had completely changed his mind and that meant work.

He had changed it less from what he had seen than the manner in which the deed had been done. There'd been none of the joy of rampaging destruction but a cold, impersonal, calculated savagery. He had seen nothing like it himself for years, not since he'd chosen to join the Free French and he'd been clawing his way up the spine of Italy against a determined and brutally desperate enemy. He still sent a card of thanks every Christmas to the young British major who'd saved a stranger from summary court martial and shooting.

He had seen nothing to compete till this morning. Enjoyment was the pulse of that Market? Well, perhaps it was but not in fever. There were men there who would use arms mercilessly.

His doubts had dissolved but not his fears. His doubts had been of this people's potential but his fears had come from Henshawe's hints of another more potent organisation.

He wrote a signal to his deputy who was keeping his seat warm whilst he was away. He didn't have Abdel's standing or subtlety but he was reliable and completely loyal. *Not interested in unfriendly neighbour's known operations in Northern Ireland but grateful to know at once if he has been sending money, or arms, or both to England and if so to what organisation.*

Abdel gave this to a clerk to encypher, telling him that any answer should be brought to his flat if it came at night.

He was woken at four o'clock in the morning.

Strong suspicion and some evidence that the person referred to has been sending substantial sums of money to the Foundation for the Advancement of African Rights (FAAR). It is one of several similar bleeding hearts set-ups but is also the front for a professional

62

subversionist called John Heyton Carr, now passing under the name of Ahab. Carr was imprisoned in this country in 1973. Escaped 1974, killing two jailers. Went on to Greece where he was roughly handled. But it is believed that our neighbour has been hesitating before committing himself to the despatch of actual weapons without proof of an organisation completely ready to use them.

Abdelaziz got up and made himself tea since he knew that further sleep was impossible. He sat in a chair, stony-faced and motionless. So this Ahab had the men but not the arms. Henshawe didn't have men but he did have weapons.

There was going to be trouble and this wasn't his country.

The three young thugs were defiant but frightened. Ahab had not suggested they sit and they stood before his desk in a sulky line. He was an ex-wrestler who had been billed as *The Scholar* for he held a very fair degree from a university still considered respectable. As a wrestler he was over the top, his skullcap of wiry hair was thinning, the hard fat on his stomach turning to soft. But he was still an enormously powerful man who could have thrown any two of them out of the window. He sat in his shirt-sleeves, his waistcoat open. He was also in a towering rage.

"You're a pack of incompetent fools," he said. "I don't hire you to beat up Indian restaurants."

One of them ventured a question. "How did you know?"

Ahab looked at him. "Do you really think you're the only ones? If you do you're even worse fools than I thought."

"Then somebody grassed on us?"

"Somebody did what I pay him to do. Which is more than you did." Ahab was quieter and therefore more formidable. "Now listen carefully. I pay you to do the rough stuff quietly, to hold the Saviours together when anyone wavers. Smashing up Wogs isn't part of that."

The middle man in the row plucked up courage. "The police haven't been to us."

"Wait to say it."

"And even if they did we wouldn't talk."

63

"Wait to say that too, my friend. The police can be very persuasive indeed."

"Anyway they haven't been."

The answer set Ahab off again. So far he hadn't sworn but now he did; he swore with panache and in several languages; he hit at them where it hurt, which was money. None of them had a regular job but in their own society they were regarded as princes. Ahab paid well and he paid on the nail.

"If this happens again you're out for good. And you know what will happen then? I'll tell you. You'll commit some petty crime and get caught. You'll have to court your girls instead of just flashing your roll."

He could see that he was getting home. The talk of crime had not impressed them but the talk of women had cut to the quick. They had only to snap their fingers and not at tarts. Without money they'd just be three unemployed layabouts.

"I'll turn a blind eye once but never again."

When they had gone Ahab smiled sardonically. There was much he would have liked to ask them but they hadn't the brains to do more than bring gossip. For hard news he had to rely on Barbara whom he'd planted on Michael Henshawe three weeks ago. She had gone without complaint, even happily, a willing martyr to what she believed her Cause. He laughed aloud: she was silly but useful. He would speak to her later and date her that evening. He hadn't a shadow of doubt she would come. His degree had been in a pseudo-science but it had taught him how to read the Barbaras.

Michael Henshawe cooked a tinned supper irritably. Barbara had given her word that this evening she would be back for certain and now it was eleven o'clock. She hadn't even bothered to telephone. He knew it would be another man but he didn't bother to guess who he was. She would do for the time, bless her twisted guts, and that was all he could reasonably ask of her.

Chapter 6

Barbara Rhys-Harte had passed a fairly typical morning. Her title at FAAR was executive secretary and her first business was to filter the mail, which ranged from what was boringly frivolous to matters which could be used in the Cause. FAAR didn't look for its raw material: it poured in in an ill-tempered stream. All over London were similar workers, most of them with a second income, each with his own special Aunt Sally. These were the targets of the progressive establishment – the prison officers, stipendiary magistrates and, easily at the top of the list, the corrupt and fascist, the hated police. All of these busy bees used the same technique: where there wasn't a case which a court would take seriously there was always the innuendo, the smear.

She threw away some begging letters and some others whose writers wanted a job, leaving herself with three for serious thought. The first was a report of an amateur football match. The teams had not been of great importance but one of them had been commendably mixed and the referee, white, had sent off a black. He had complained at once of discrimination and now had written to FAAR to urge his case. Barbara reluctantly shook her head. She could send a report to the official commission and receive in return a carefully-phrased letter asking for further information. Had the referee previously warned the man? There was a code which governed sendings-off, particularly in amateur matches, so was there any evidence that this code had been breached to the man's disadvantage?

So Barbara shook her head but not in despair; she had another resource and intended to use it. That resource was the unanswerable smear. There was a man on telly who ran a feature on football; he was sympathetic to FAAR and an excellent actor who would know how to handle the story perfectly – the change of tone and the look of pain. The unthinking viewer would hardly doubt that injustice had taken place and gone unpunished.

The next case was a little more promising, for a West Indian had tried to join the police. The police would have been delighted to have him but he was three inches too short and myopic to the point of near blindness. And of course this was surely very unfair. They would say that rules were rules, the same for all. But they shouldn't be the same for all. A West Indian was entitled to have them bent for him. Not to do so was discrimination.

She considered how to handle this one, deciding to send it to Mrs Alderney Cohn. Mrs Alderney Cohn had a friend in parliament and he could present it as an awkward question. Of course there would be a solid answer but a tiny doubt would be left to fester.

All grist to the sacred mill.

Her third case was the best of all, the pearl of a morning's conscientious beastliness. It was a clipping from a reputable newspaper, the same which James Bullen had passed to Russell. A chief constable had levelled a very serious charge against what the paper had called the race relations industry, daring to say that it had been infiltrated by agitators whose express purpose was to increase tension rather than decrease it.

Barbara Rhys-Harte was angry for this statement broke all the contemporary rules. They were the rules of silence, of looking away from it. You might suspect such a thing but you mustn't say it. If you did you'd be immediately ostracised from any society of right-thinking people. She knew enough of the current climate of thought, of the power which her industry slyly exploited, to make a very good guess at what had happened. This chief constable would have been sent a letter. It might have been anything from a flaming rocket to an admonition from some assistant secretary. But it appeared that he hadn't been sacked on the spot and that was clearly quite intolerable.

This was the hottest potato for weeks and she wondered how to handle it best. To put it before the whole board of FAAR would be the orthodox course, and therefore the safest. But it would also be the least effective. The board met monthly but did very little. The bishop of Crondal was there for his name; he took very little practical interest and in any case had absorbing hobbies. Lord Welcome-Wills was close to gaga. He was passable till about half-past eleven but after he'd had his morning gins he might have been

66

on another planet. And it was a little beyond Mrs Cohn's earnest righteousness.

Barbara decided she'd put it to Ahab. He'd been away a lot lately, he often was, but he was coming in later this morning at lunchtime.

She smiled as she considered Ahab. How many people knew the truth, that FAAR was being used as a front by a man whose end was straightforward subversion? Not Welcome-Wills, he was far too senile, and the bishop of Crondal wouldn't care. Mrs Alderney Cohn? Well, she might suspect, but she was one of a dozen similar ladies to whom mischief was the air they breathed. She'd been in mischief since she had learnt to walk and she wasn't choosey about what mischief, provided it kept her name in the newspapers. So here Ahab was, officially the office manager, an office manager who was often absent. Nobody seemed to notice much but Barbara kept a careful file of his very obliging doctor's certificates.

He was late and came in well after lunchtime and, as he walked past her desk, he nodded absently. He had something on his mind – she knew that face. Nevertheless she stopped him as he went by.

"There's something here I'd like to show you."

He hesitated but finally said: "Bring it into my room, please."

They went to it. It was pokey and the desk was dusty but an office manager had a room to himself. He read the cutting but his face didn't change. Barbara, who was excited, said:

"What do we do about that?"

"We do nothing." He seemed to be taking it surprisingly calmly. "Something like this was bound to happen and it's happened at the worst time possible. Just as we're getting close to a crisis. If we complain we'll only give it publicity. At this moment that's the last thing sensible." He could see she was deflated and smiled. "I'm sorry if I've disappointed you. Come to my place again this evening. I'll make it up."

"All right," she said flatly; she wasn't thrilled. But she thought of her great-grandfather flogging his slaves. In fact he had been humane and considerate but her picture of his way of life had set her feet on this path and would keep them there steadily. And Ahab's technique in bed was abrasive. She was experienced with men and could take it but it annoyed her that he seemed to be proud of it. He seemed to believe she liked it rough whereas she liked it with flowers and a schmaltzy string orchestra. But every time she lay with Ahab a tiny part of her debt was paid, a tiny part of her secret guilt healed.

She woke next morning alone in bed, listening to Ahab shave and shower. He didn't always do that first thing and she could recognise the signal clearly. For a moment her face fell but then recovered. She was here for her strictly private therapy and if the doctor ordered a double dose she wasn't the sort of patient to decline.

Somewhere half-way between sleep and waking she considered the two men she was lying with. She had been planted by Ahab on Michael Henshawe to watch his actions, not to assess his character, but in the weeks that she had spent with him she had been able to form her own opinion. He was a man with an enormous compulsion (she had heard the word, but preferred chip on shoulder) and that chip was a hatred of all things British. She couldn't think why since it didn't seem necessary. She knew that he was Anglo-Irish and that his family had once been wealthy. Now they were not but that wasn't exceptional. The word gentleman was nowadays suspect, there were people who looked away if you used it, but that was what he was inescapably; and the impoverished Anglo-Irish gentry had for centuries had an open escape route. They went into the British army which was very glad indeed to receive them. But if you mentioned the army to Michael he froze. Barbara thought of him with a sort of tolerance but if he was trying to bust the British he hadn't a hope or anything like it. Despite the Rhys in her name she wasn't Welsh – nothing since that appalling great-grandfather – and the Celtic twilight was not her climate.

Ahab was entirely different, as positive as a kick in the stomach. It was difficult to guess his provenance but she knew that he had been in America. Yet his accent wasn't the drawl of the South and certainly not a Western whine; it was more like the acrid twang of St Louis. Perhaps he'd been born there and maybe not but in either case he had suffered much trouble. A powerful organisation had marked him, following him from state to state, and finally he

68

had had to leave. He had lived in several countries since, and in Greece they had pulled him in and tortured him. He had showed her his broken right hand to prove it and he still used his left to write laboriously. And always he had been seeking his goal.

What was it? For all his drive she wasn't quite sure. He didn't want a multi-racial society, he regarded that as a liberal chimera, but sometimes after venery he would talk to her as an accepted equal. She knew he had been to a university and she didn't always understand him ... Anarchism had a respectable pedigree, the world must be made again whatever the cost. Despite her name, Barbara was English and she had thought this dangerously near to mysticism. But whatever it was, the man was possessed by it. Of the three of them he alone had discipline. Beside him Henshawe was a dilettante and she herself just a girl with a sense of guilt.

He came in now and surprised her greatly for he had brought her a cup of tea on a tray. Normally she had to make her own. He put it on the bed and sat down. He was wearing a multi-coloured dressing gown which Barbara thought vulgar but didn't say so. He was also in an unusual temper, good-humoured and in his strange way gentle.

"I'm sorry I was short at lunchtime – I mean about that bloody chief constable. I would have said I was sorry before but I forgot." He gave her his wide smile. "There were other things."

"You were perfectly right. We don't want publicity." She said 'we' because they slept together, knowing she wasn't really in, hoping that in the mood which now rode him he might relax his accustomed unbroken reticence.

He did so but began obliquely. "You've done well," he said. "I'm very grateful."

She was pleased and showed it. "I've not found out much."

"You've found out two things of great importance. The first is that Henshawe is often away. Do you know where he goes or what he does?"

"No, I haven't found out that."

"Then I'll tell you. He's trying to compete with me."

"At what?"

"You know I'm forming black cells in the cities?"

"I'd guessed it," she said. "I'm not quite stupid."

69

"Of course he hasn't a hope of doing it. He sets something up and I knock it down. I'm a professional: Henshawe isn't. He has money from somewhere but so have I." He hesitated but finally said it. "What I do not have are arms."

"And Henshawe has?"

"You're quick this morning. No, I didn't say that but I think it's possible."

"Anything to go on?"

"Quicker than ever. Two things as it happens, one mine one yours. The first is various hints he's been dropping. Nothing definite, you know, just come-ons. To men he thought were his but were mine."

"And the other thing – the one I gave you?"

"That furniture van. Tell me that again."

She hadn't thought it of any consequence but collected her thoughts and re-told the story. "He stayed up late one night and it called for him. I was in bed but got out and peeked. It was a furniture van with two blacks in the front of it."

"Did you recognise them?"

"I'd never seen them."

"And the name of the van had been painted out?"

"That was the impression I got but there were only street-lights. I can't be sure."

"And Henshawe went off in the van with the blacks?"

She nodded but she risked a question. "But why is that van important?"

"It may not be. But vans can be used to transport arms."

"A pretty long shot."

"I've had to make them before."

He brought her another cup of tea and this time one for himself as well. "I'm asking a shocking lot of questions." This wasn't his normal form and she liked it.

"I'm doing my best with the shocking answers."

"I suppose he's never mentioned guns?"

"You suppose quite right. Why ever should he?"

"Have you ever asked him?"

She said reasonably, "Until this morning I never knew of them."

70

"Will you ask him now?"

"I will if you wish. It sounds perfectly hopeless."

"Again a very long shot but not hopeless. Men talk in bed and sometimes after it. As I am now," he added quietly.

"I will if you ask."

"I'm sure you can be very persuasive."

She didn't much like it but let it pass. "Won't it make him suspicious?"

"You're thinking well. Of course it will make him suspicious. That I accept."

"Suppose he just denies the whole thing?"

"Then we're back to where we are at this moment, waiting for something to break. As I'm sure it will. Not something he does but something done to him."

"You're full of hunches this morning."

"Yes, I am. I've a hunch there's going to be a development and I've a hunch that Henshawe does have hardware." He rose and kissed her forehead gently. He had never done that before and she was touched. "Now back to Henshawe and keep me posted."

"Just as master says," she said.

He replied on a note she hadn't heard. "I don't think you'll have to stay with him long."

"That suits me fine. He isn't my type."

"I never thought he was."

"You're a bastard."

The doorbell rang at six the next evening and Michael Henshawe went to open it. A handsome woman stood outside it. "I'm Anne Bullen," she said.

"But you've got your head on."

"It grew again."

"I'm delighted to see it."

There had been the immediate spark of congeniality. "And I'm not selling vacuum cleaners or brushes."

"I didn't suppose you were. Please come in."

She did so and sat on the sofa gracefully. Michael Henshawe asked: "Would you like a drink?"

"What have you got ?"

"I've got some whisky."

"I like it half and half with water. No ice, please." The manner was polite but decided.

Henshawe poured and, as he did so, observed her. He saw a woman in her early thirties dressed in a classical coat and skirt, wearing a string of pearls which might be real. He noticed, too, that she wore no wedding ring but the deduction from this would have been misleading. She had in fact been married off young by an impoverished father who had been glad to get rid of her. Her husband had been a good deal older and also, though rich, decidedly mean. The match had been neither fruitful nor happy and when he had died she had wished to forget it. She had taken off her wedding ring and reverted to her maiden name. Her husband's had been unpronounceably Scottish and he as dour as his northern moors which she still rented out at inflated prices to Americans who shot them to pieces. Now she was catching up on life with a flat and a car and discreet entertainment. From time to time she took a lover and one of the first of these had been Russell. Twice she had been able to help him and her brother still worked for Charles Russell's successor.

She took a long pull at the whisky and said: "I've come from the Security Executive." She saw him stiffen and wasn't surprised: people did stiffen when you mentioned the Executive. "I'm a persuader but I don't carry a cosh."

"Then what is your weapon?"

"A smooth tongue and I would hope some charm."

He laughed at that – she had meant him to do so. "What are you trying to persuade me to do?"

"To talk to the Security Executive."

"And why should I do that?"

She visibly collected herself. The Executive had trusted her and the Executive had not been idle. From the starting point of Michael Henshawe they had worked their way, through Barbara Rhys-Harte, to the Foundation which they had guessed was a front. But they hadn't had pressing need to discover for what. Now, following the trail, they had, and the discovery had set them back on their heels. There were reports on Ahab from four different countries and none of them made him welcome in Britain.

She began to spell it out in order. "The Executive knows you have arms," she said. "Quite a lot of them and they don't approve."

"Then I'd be putting my head in a noose to go near them."

She told him much what Abdel once had. "The Executive is not the police. They can't hold or arrest you or even charge you. But they can be very dangerous enemies."

"Is that a threat?"

"I prefer 'advice'."

A trifle drily he said: "You're very kind."

She took it without offence. "Not kind. I'm generously paid for what I'm doing and if I bring it off there's a bonus."

"Which you need?"

"Frankly, no."

He laughed again; he was liking this woman. Either she was playing it straight or else she was a superlative actress. In either case he greatly admired her. He would play along a little longer.

"So I go to your Executive and there I earn myself a grilling."

"I wouldn't say that – say a friendly chat. I've a brother who works there. I know the form."

"And it's this brother I shall be seeing?"

"I doubt it. He's a backroom boy. He doesn't go out on jobs or see callers."

"Then who will conduct this astonishing interview?" Again there was more than a hint of sarcasm and once again she ignored it blandly.

"I don't know that and I don't pretend to but it will probably be what they call an operator. And the one they might choose may surprise you greatly."

"Why should it do that?"

"Because he's black. And extremely civilised."

"It sounds interesting but it's hardly enough. Not enough for the very evident risk."

She played her big card with practised smoothness. "They might offer you something more than a civilised chat."

"What could they?"

"Something you need very badly. Protection."

"Come clean."

"I intend to. Besides following you wherever you go the Executive has been doing its homework. It does, you know – it's extremely efficient."

"So I have always heard. And so?"

Her manner became a shade more formal. The hand was going her way and she played cards well. "You are living with a girl called Rhys-Harte."

He nodded. There was no point in denial.

"Who works for something called FAAR."

"I know."

Anne Bullen said coolly: "The girl is a plant."

She had him now, he was seriously interested.

"A plant by whom?"

"Have you heard of a man called Ahab?"

"No . . . Yes. Barbara mentioned him once, I think. He has some sort of job in FAAR himself."

"Which he uses as his cover."

"For what?"

"For his ambition to stand the world on its head."

"The Executive *has* been doing its homework. But why should he want to plant on me?"

"To find out all she could about your job."

"It was prettily done. I met her socially."

"Would it surprise you to know where she spent last night?"

"Nothing would surprise me now."

"Ahab and you have two things in common. The first is a taste for criminal mischief, the second that you both take money from foreign powers. But yours has sent you weapons too and as far as we know Ahab's has not. So if he even suspects that you have arms he'll go for them through you and not gently." She rose confidently. "Are you coming?"

"Yes."

She had a car outside and they drove to the Executive. At the door she said:

"My job ends here."

"If I may say so you did it well." He hesitated. "Will you have lunch with me?"

"It isn't against any rule I know of." She gave him her address

74

and he went upstairs.

A lean West Indian rose as he entered the room; he bowed politely. "Mr Michael Henshawe? My name is William Wilberforce Smith and I'm what this business calls an operator."

"Unlike Miss Bullen's brother who works behind blinds."

"That is correct." Willy waved at a chair and Henshawe took it. There were cigarettes on the table and Willy offered one.

"Thank you. I don't smoke."

"You're lucky. I smoke a bit of pot occasionally but so far I haven't got hooked."

"Just as well in your job."

"That again is correct."

Henshawe had been trying to place Willy. He was expensively dressed and he spoke without accent. Henshawe recognised his tie.

. . . Beware.

"May I ask why I've been brought here?"

"Certainly. In the first place to hear a strictly formal complaint."

"Of what?"

"Of the fact that the other night you shot at me."

Henshawe was silent and Willy smiled. "You mustn't get me wrong, you know. We're not the police and I've been shot at before. I said the complaint was strictly formal but we know what was in that pillbox, though not where you moved them."

"Which you think you might twist out of me?"

"Nothing so foolish. You are here to receive a proposition."

"Then make it and get it over."

"I will. Did Miss Bullen mention a man called Ahab?" Henshawe nodded.

"I'm glad she didn't forget – we asked her to." Willy seemed to hesitate though in fact he had his next sentences pat. "I'm going to say something which may offend you. You're competent – you proved that that evening – but you're simply not in Ahab's class. If anybody is holding those weapons we'd very much rather you did it than he."

"If *you* can't find them how can *he*?"

"He can do what we can't – beat them out of you."

75

"I can take a beating."

Willy Smith sighed. He had heard tales of unbelievable fortitude, of men and even a couple of women who had defied the Gestapo and kept their secrets. William Wilberforce Smith did not believe them: Charles Russell had told him not to do so. "Nevertheless I will make my offer. Ahab is a hard old pro – how hard I sincerely hope you'll never find out. As far as we know Ahab doesn't have arms. You have. So long as that's so you're in personal danger."

. . . He's bluffing of course, but I'll hear him out.

"So tell us where those arms are and we'll deal with them. The police will not be involved directly, certainly not against yourself. When we have the arms we'll have done what we're paid to. Meanwhile you will have proper protection."

"From this Ahab? You exaggerate."

"No."

Michael Henshawe rose. "Am I free to go?"

"Of course you are free to go. Good night."

When Henshawe had gone Willy sighed again softly. The hook hadn't struck but he still had work to do. He had offered protection as part of a bargain and that bargain had been turned down flat. But he'd been speaking the truth when he'd said he feared Ahab and he must still forfend his most likely action. Which was to snatch Michael Henshawe and force him to talk.

He picked up a phone and gave crisp clear orders. The tail could still be left on Henshawe though he wouldn't go near the hardware – he dare not. But two competent guards were to be put on him instantly and if anything happened to Henshawe they'd lose their jobs.

Barbara had had a tiresome morning for the board had held its monthly meeting and she had had to attend and record the minutes. What a sham they all were, she thought – what sillies. The bishop of Crondal was very low church but took a very high church view of race. God had made men in His sacred image so even to think that one race might be lesser was an insult to the Godhead directly. This doctrine he preached with a show of conviction but it didn't seem to affect his way of life. He lent his reputation to FAAR, that reputation being way-out progressive, but he did nothing more than attend its meetings. Lord Welcome-Wills had attended too and the meeting had to be held at ten thirty since for an hour after that his lordship could cope. Dimly but he could just about cope. But at half-past eleven he would start on the gin and after that he was over the hill, irrecoverable. Only Mrs Alderney Cohn might have an inkling of what went on in FAAR's shadow. Barbara had seen her look at Ahab, a curious look almost conspiratorial, and she treated him with a certain deference. She hadn't Barbara's helpless commitment but she could turn a very blind eye and did so.

Barbara stayed late with her minutes, then took a taxi to Henshawe's flat. The living room door was closed for once but she could hear that Henshawe was using the telephone. She slipped into the bedroom silently, picking up the extension carefully, hoping that no click would betray her. She didn't know the voice at the other end. It spoke good English but not an Englishman's.

"They've had time to tap your line by now."

"I'm saying nothing they don't already know. In any case I'll have to risk it. This is urgent and you've got to know."

"On your own head be it." Abdel was not distressed for himself. He knew he was suspected of killing Maoui and he'd been seen in a public house with Henshawe. Against that he was an accredited diplomat. He'd be difficult to touch but Henshawe was not.

"I've been called to the Security Executive."

"You do not surprise me. Whom did you see?"

"A man called William Wilberforce Smith."

"He's one of their up-and-comers. What did he say?"

"They know I have weapons."

"But not yet where."

"So it seems. But they also made me a proposition. Have you heard of a man called Ahab?"

"I have." Barbara could hear that the voice had sharpened.

"The Executive takes this Ahab seriously. What he is up to they didn't tell me in terms, but they told me that since arms existed they'd prefer them in my hands than see them in his."

"And the proposition they made you?"

"Was very simple. Whatever his plan is this Ahab needs arms.

77

And the Executive thought he would go for ours. By going for me and beating them out of me."

"That was typical Security thinking."

"So if I told them where the stuff was hidden they'd collect it and forget the whole thing. As a bonus they would protect me from Ahab."

The voice said grimly: "You may very well need it. What happened then?"

"I turned it down and came home to ring you. They didn't attempt to detain me."

"They wouldn't."

There was a silence while the unknown man thought. Abdel was in fact approving. He was bound to his father by chains of *pietas* and Henshawe for his part had eaten salt. And he hadn't betrayed it though he must have been tempted. He must know he was both in a muddle and danger, the plan he had accepted impractical, the risks to himself unexpected and menacing. Abdelaziz smiled his dour hillman's smile. He too had his doubts of his father's plan, but whatever the outcome he'd stand by Henshawe.

It was Henshawe who finally broke the silence. "And one other thing though it's less important. That girl I've been living with is Ahab's plant."

"But you've told her nothing?"

"Nothing whatever."

The voice at the other end said: "I must think."

Barbara Rhys-Harte didn't hesitate for she'd been blown and was no longer useful. She packed a couple of suitcases quickly and went into the living room carrying them. Henshawe was in a chair and said mildly:

"Going away for a bit?"

"For good."

He gave her a look of unconcealed hatred but all he said was: "That's just as well."

She had a small flat of her own which her mother paid for and there she packed another suitcase. Then she took a taxi and gave Ahab's address. She had forgotten about her secret penance. She was simply going back to Ahab. Perhaps she could even teach him to be less rough.

78

Chapter 7

Barbara Rhys-Harte slept late next morning as indeed she had some need to do. Ahab had been indefatigable, spurred mercilessly by some ancient god she didn't know. But she hadn't had to teach or persuade him for the abrasiveness, the need to impose his will, had gone. He'd been tender and surprisingly catholic and she waited in the warm bed in contentment.

Again he brought her tea on a tray but this time the pot, two cups and milk. It was a larger tray and he handled it awkwardly. She could see his right hand was almost useless. He had shown it to her to prove he'd been tortured but he had never told her the story of why. He was looking at it with a sort of contempt and she said to relax him:

"Care to tell?"

To her surprise he answered at once and easily. "It was in Greece as I told you but it wasn't the colonels. I was after bigger game than the colonels, I was after the man who set them up and financed them. He was a shipping tycoon, an especially nasty one. I made a slip and his hard men grabbed me. It went on and on and on and on. I don't have the special sort of courage which can stand a great deal of pain indefinitely. I broke early but they didn't believe me – it sounded preposterous. So on it went till they simply got tired of it. After that the regular police threw me out. That was something I've got thoroughly used to."

Ahab was entirely bilingual; he could talk like a man on commercial telly trying to coax his wife into changing the cooker or he could talk standard mid-Atlantic effortlessly. This morning it was the mid-Atlantic with a hint of the academic to give it salt. Barbara was beginning to know him and she recognised the omen as favourable. Emboldened she said:

"You've lived a hard life."

"I've obeyed what the jargon calls my imperatives."

"Are you a communist?"

"Certainly not."

"An anarchist?"

He thought it over. "The word must do. But you cannot do the sort of things I do if your only food is a political philosophy. You've got to feel it here." He touched his stomach.

"What sort of things?" She was getting still bolder.

"Killing, for instance."

"You've killed a man?"

"Several. I go for the big ones, the really corrupt. Like that Greek shipping magnate I didn't get. But in Bolivia my time wasn't wasted – the people behind the tin mines are careless – and in France there was a police chief, an animal. But two killings I regret and bitterly. I was pulled in once in a state in North Africa and to escape I had to kill two jailors. I did it with my hands before one was spoiled. They were working men doing their job and I feel ashamed."

"And whom do you plan to kill in England?" She knew she was pushing her luck but he answered.

"Nobody. This is the big one."

"How big?"

"Revolution."

Revolutions happened in Central America or in Russia's European empire where they were promptly crushed and by the wise man forgotten. "Revolution in England?" She didn't believe him.

"Why not? It's ripe for it. The intellectual Left is impotent but the blacks could go up in flame at the touch of a match."

She was getting out of her depth and said: "I don't understand what drives you."

"Nor do I." He kissed her on the forehead again. "But I think I understand what drives you." He poured her another cup of tea. "You're trying to work something out of your system."

"You're cleverer than the average headshrinker."

"And are you succeeding."

"Last night helped a lot."

"So I can see," he said coolly but he smiled.

He was in a very rare mood of relaxation and now he began to reflect aloud. "So here the three of us are – you, me and Henshawe – all driven by different motives but tangled together."

"I don't think Henshawe's driven at all. Not in the sense that you are or even me."

He was interested. "Then what makes him tick?"

"He's as bitter as aloes and wants revenge. He loathes everything English but the hate is –"

"Well?"

She had found her word. "The hate is unfocused."

"He must be a very unhappy man."

"He's that all right but he isn't negligible. He might almost be like you but for one thing."

"And what is that?"

"He's stuffed with self-pity."

It was his turn to say: "You're clever this morning."

"I'm a woman, aren't I?"

"I have reason to know it."

She stretched like a cat and he said at once: "I'll go and shave."

"You needn't bother."

When it was finished she heard him showering. He came back and picked up the tea-tray clumsily. "You must be hungry," he said.

"How did you know?"

"If you weren't you would be abnormal. You are not."

"Thank you, dear doctor."

"You're a pleasure to treat. I prescribe eggs and bacon and rather a lot of them. I'll go and do them while you get up."

She ate ravenously and in total silence, watching him eat well but rather less. His dark skullcap of wiry hair was still wet and his splendid white teeth tore the food to pieces. She guessed that he hadn't always had enough.

She started to wash up but he stopped her. "We ought to discuss what you heard last night."

That hadn't been Barbara's idea of the morning. It was Sunday, they could do as they liked, and she had wanted to listen to some of his records. She had thought he would like New Orleans or reggae, but no, his meat was red-blooded opera, *Tosca* in particular, preferably with Callas and Gobbi. She had seen him sit and listen intently, his body as taut as a bow but in bliss. Or perhaps she could persuade him to come to church. She still clung to a vague and spineless religion and there was a church nearby which was more Romish than Rome, bells and smells and gorgeous apparel, boys' voices and a thundering organ. Barbara went there sometimes as free theatre.

But she could see that he wanted to talk and left the kitchen. In the living room he sat down firmly, as solid as a truck and as direct. "So there *are* arms," he said. "That's proven now."

"And Henshawe has them."

"Till I take them from him. That I always hoped to do but now there's a more urgent priority. That's the man Henshawe saw when they called him up."

"That William Wilberforce Smith? Why's he important?"

"Because he's black."

"How do you know that?"

She could see that she had come close to irritating him but he gave her a good-tempered answer. "The establishment of the Security Executive isn't published in any government list but if, like me, you need to know it you can find it out, at least in outline. The head is a man called Pallant, an ex-policeman. Under him are what they call the operators and behind them are the researchers, the backroom boys. This Smith is a highly professional operator, and as I told you he is also black." He could see that she hadn't clicked and went on. "In south London I have one of my biggest cells but it is also one of the least secure. I even have to pay thugs to keep it together. A clever black might infiltrate; he might learn what he shouldn't and not only of London. In which case those weapons hardly matter since there wouldn't be the men to use them. The Executive would break up my cells."

"That was always a risk," she said.

"You're smarter than I thought you were but you still haven't got the essential point. A clever black could infiltrate, certainly, but how many blacks has the other side got? A policeman or two but they'd be spotted at once. And in the Executive there is only this Smith." He rose and began to pace the room. "This Willy Smith is an immediate threat, more important for the moment than the arms. This Willy Smith must be put out of action." He had returned to his chair, his eyes unwavering; he seemed to be assessing her will. Finally he said:

82

"You could serve."

She liked the word, it was one between equals. It avoided the very evident differences but it emphasised what they held in common.

"I don't think I could kill a man."

"I'm sure you couldn't – I wasn't suggesting it. In any case there's no need to kill. A fortnight off duty will do as well." He seemed to be changing the subject but wasn't. "I believe you once knew a man called James Bullen, one of the Executive's backroom boys."

She risked his irritation again. "How did you know?"

But this time Ahab showed no annoyance. "A perfectly reasonable question – I'll answer it. Naturally I checked on you before I took you into my bed and confidence." He saw her look of offence and added: "After all, you might have been planted on me as I planted you on Michael Henshawe."

She wasn't quite happy but let it pass. "It's all over between me and Bullen."

"Do you still sometimes see him?"

"I've met him once or twice at parties. We talk of the weather and leave it at that."

Very British, he thought – very English indeed. "Would he see you if you asked him to?"

"I just don't know."

"What sort of man is he?"

She thought carefully before she answered. "Ex-Army type. Conscientious. Dutiful. He might feel he had an obligation."

"Then he'll see you all right." Ahab spoke with total confidence. "So you go to him showing reluctance but also distress. You've heard talk of arms and you do not like it. He'll react to that – it's his job to do so."

"And after that?"

"Let him appear to drag it out of you. You've a clue where the arms are hidden – I'll write it down. Of course they'll move to check at once, but they won't send Bullen, he isn't an operator. They'll send the man on the case, this Willy Smith. And we shall be waiting for Willy Smith."

He could see that he was pulling her two ways, between the urge

83

to help him in any way possible and the knowledge that a man would be hurt. At last she said:

"A fortnight off duty, I think you said."

"There's an axiom about minimum force."

She repeated his earlier question to her. "What sort of man is he?"

"Rich and well-educated. An Uncle Tom."

"I'll do it," she said; she hadn't hesitated for it was the worst name she knew. She had a private league table of West Indian virtue. At the top were the banausics, the labourers, the men on the roads or on building sites who got cruelly and unjustly sacked when they broke some piece of expensive machinery. One class less deserving were the good-steady-jobbers, the men who worked on the railways or buses, and one below them were the traders and shopkeepers who sometimes made a comfortable living. At the bottom were a handful of soldiers and the men who worked in white men's clubs and often seemed quite proud to do so. These were the Uncle Toms, the dregs.

Or had been up to this moment. Not now. To her private demonology had been added something she hadn't thought of, the successful black who worked for the enemy. "I'll do it," she said again. "The man's a traitor."

He looked at her and he hid a smile. She was quick enough but very shallow. He rose and wrote on a piece of paper. "That's the address where the arms are. Or rather aren't. Try to fix your date with Bullen round about six. The Executive will react pretty promptly and by seven o'clock it's nicely dark. Ring me as soon as you've made your date with him."

James Bullen had been surprised when Barbara telephoned. She had sounded distressed, and as she herself had correctly told Ahab he had a powerful sense of obligation. He saw the problem first as practical, of where to meet without embarrassment. If he took her to a restaurant there was the outside chance that Pallant would hear of it and if he did so he wouldn't let it go by . . . So he *was* still seeing Barbara, was he? That would be bad but it would be worse to have lied. In the end he accepted the lesser risk, asking her to come round to his flat. He had been strongly attracted but not

84

strongly enough and in the choice between Barbara Rhys-Harte and his work he hadn't been stretched to choose the latter.

Barbara had guessed this and wasn't flattered. No woman was ever quite the same when the man had been the one to end it and moreover she had resented the manner. For he had done it with aplomb, rather skilfully. There'd been no sudden denouement or flaming row, no refusing to answer her calls on the telephone, but a calculated decrease in the meetings until finally there had been none at all. She was going to see him now to fool him, possibly to land him in serious trouble, but she would have confessed that the knowledge was not unwelcome. The break in their relationship, which for once in her life had been less than total, had been too smoothly manoeuvred, too calmly accepted. A certain malice added an edge to her duty.

So now she sat on his sofa demurely. She was soberly dressed and had already declined a drink politely. He had decided his line which was to go at it straight. The sooner this was over the better.

"I gather you're in some trouble. What can I do?"

She too had decided how to handle it and she wasn't going to take it so fast. "You remember I work in FAAR?"

"Of course."

"I've been finding out things I'd rather not have."

"Such as what?"

"It's being used as a front."

James Bullen appeared to be thinking it over: in fact he was making a fresh decision. She was going to tell him things he knew. Should he in turn disclose that he knew them? He decided to let her talk on and said:

"If it is it isn't the only one like it."

"You know what I feel about blacks in this country. I feel passionately that they've had a raw deal."

"Or you wouldn't be working for FAAR," he said.

"But I didn't join it to stir up violence." She seemed to be hesitating but in fact was timing it. "Have you heard of a man called Ahab?"

"Yes." If he said 'No' she would hardly believe him. He was on to something here; he mustn't stop her.

"You know what he does?"

"We have had reports."

"He's entitled to fight for social justice."

Jesus, he thought, she's swallowed that too, but all he said was: "As you yourself do."

"But I didn't join FAAR to fight to break the law."

He reverted to his first directness. "Is it being broken?"

"I think so." There was another carefully-timed hesitation. "That's why I've come to you for help."

"What makes you suspicious?"

"I've seen things I shouldn't."

She could see that he was sniffing the bait but she wouldn't strike till he'd taken the hook. "Organised protest is perfectly legal but organised rioting is not."

"Quite so." He felt a little let down since he knew of the cells but he was a disciplined, conscientious listener.

"Especially," she said softly, "with guns."

He sat up straight. "Guns, did you say?"

She had him now, he had swallowed the lot, and he would gobble down anything else she fed him. But it wouldn't be good technique just to slap it down.

"The point is that I won't have them *used* – the blacks, I mean, for some political purpose which has nothing to do with their legitimate grievances."

He ignored this piece of rhetoric coolly. He wasn't interested in her private motives, the girl was a fool and they weren't worth considering, but the slightest clue to those arms was vital. He changed gear again and asked her quietly:

"Do you think that Ahab has arms?"

"Not quite. But I think he knows where arms are hidden. I told you I'd seen things I shouldn't."

"If I'm going to help you you've got to come clean."

"You won't mention my name?"

"I can't promise that but I see no need to." He added with a touch of pomposity: "We don't normally disclose our sources."

"So I think Ahab knows where arms are hidden."

"You told me that."

"And I think I know where."

He sat rigidly in his chair, unspeaking. The least mistake now, the wrong voice, the wrong question and he'd lose the biggest fish of his life.

The seconds ticked by till she finally said: "I'd rather you had those guns than Ahab. I told you I wouldn't stand for violence."

He stayed silent but it cost him an effort. At last she said: "Take this down on paper." She had memorised the address and repeated it. James Bullen wrote it. His hand was unsteady.

"I think I need a drink. Will you join me?"

She shook her head.

"Then I'll see you out and get you a taxi. Where are you going?"

"Back to my flat."

He found her a taxi and gave the address. He had to ask her since he'd wholly forgotten it. She was now in another world which wasn't his.

Back in her flat Barbara telephoned Ahab. "He swallowed the lot," she said.

"Good girl."

James Bullen went back to the drink he needed, his nerves as highly tensed as timpani. His duty was perfectly clear and established: it was to ring Pallant at home with the utmost urgency and thereafter leave any action to him.

Which would probably be to despatch Willy Smith again.

He discovered that he was grinding his teeth. He had always been underrated unfairly – it had even been the same in the army. He'd been intelligent and had passed high from the staff college. Then two jobs as a G Two had followed, the second not quite so good as the first. Then the realisation that he wouldn't go further, he wasn't going to command his regiment. He would go back as a major and there he would stick till they threw him on the scrapheap politely and reemployed him in some un-uniformed job.

He had resigned and applied to the Security Executive which had been very pleased indeed to have him, a paper-man with a good paper-man's record.

But he hadn't been content with that, he had always believed he had untapped resources. He would have commanded his regiment well – yes, he would! – and he had longed to serve the Executive actively. He had promised himself that one day he'd show them, one day the big coup would drop on his plate, knowing in his secret heart that no such thing would ever happen.

And now it had – not a doubt of that. It stared up from that plate with a deadly temptation and there was irony to spice the dish. He had always believed that his personal file held some undeserved blot from his friendship with Barbara and here was Barbara giving the chance to expunge it.

He picked up the telephone but not to ring Pallant. He rang the Executive's duty officer.

"I'm going out on a job."

"Are you indeed."

If a doubt had been left the three words settled it, the surprise and behind it the silent question. The D.O. didn't dare to ask it for he was very much James Bullen's junior, but his tone had driven the last nail home.

James Bullen was breaking a great many rules but there was one which he did not dare to ignore.

"Take this address, please, and call me tomorrow. If there's no answer check the address."

"Understood. Good luck."

James Bullen took a gun out but put it away. It was years since he'd fired it and he wasn't a marksman. He changed his clothes and found a taxi. In it he sat quietly gloating.

He was going to show the whole damned lot of them.

The three hard men had been summoned peremptorily. They were to take a taxi and Ahab would pay. This time he didn't leave them standing; he gave them chairs but nothing to drink. There hadn't been time for a full explanation, only for orders and those had been clear. Now he was recapping decisively.

"The man will be black but is dangerous to all of us. I want him out of the way for a fortnight. Anything further than that and you're out yourselves. Now go and do as I say."

They went out in an ominous huddle, in silence.

James Bullen paid his taxi off at the corner of the long dull street. It was close to where Henshawe lived and similar, perhaps a couple of places lower in the local league of respectability. Some of the houses were still well-kept but there were more that were not and still more in decay. The street was empty – these people were earlybirds – except for the lines of ancient jalopies. Most of the windows had muslin curtains and behind them the spectral flash of telly, but in one house men were singing strongly. They were singing Gospel which Bullen disliked but at least they were making their own entertainment. Civilised man was still surviving.

Bullen's confidence had begun to fade, the adrenalin was pumping less strongly. It wasn't that he had begun to feel frightened, he was still determined to seize his chance, but the difficulties had begun to obtrude themselves. If the address was in fact some respectable couple's, he was going to look an enormous fool, and if there were a cache of arms it would be locked and very possibly guarded. He hadn't been taught to deal with locks, far less the arts of unarmed combat.

When he reached the house it reassured him on one point. For all practical purposes the place was a ruin, vandalised, boarded-up, abandoned, a natural for any sort of hideaway. He pushed at the front door and it opened. He had brought a torch and used it gingerly. There were four rooms downstairs all securely padlocked. He went up the stairs which creaked alarmingly. Again four doors and three were chained. He tried the fourth and it opened easily. He had time to see that the room was empty except for three men who rushed him silently. One of them swung a cosh and he fell.

The three young hard men stood round him, puzzled.

"Ahab said he was going to be black."

"Ahab has screwed it up."

"So what do we do?"

"We get away from here and tell him."

The tallest man said: "No. Not yet". He looked down at the unconscious Bullen. "Whitey," he said softly. "Whitey." He kicked Bullen in the ribs reflectively. He was wearing heavy boots with reinforced toes.

The eldest of the three said: "Steady."

"Whitey," the other said again. "Dear Whitey." The voice was almost a ritual chant.

The eldest was scared but not of James Bullen; he was scared of the tall man's savage temper. He turned his torch on his face and his fright increased. The tall man's eyes had begun to glaze. "Sweet Whitey," he said for the final time and kicked with all his strength at Bullen's head.

James Bullen was in one way lucky. The blow with the cosh had been heavy and accurate and he never felt the kick which split his skull.

Chapter 8

The three men sat round the table dour and grim – Jack Pallant,
Charles Russell and Willy Smith. Russell and Pallant had lost men
before but they had been operators on active missions. They had
gone voluntarily and had died with their boots on, mostly by the
gun and abroad. Neither had lost a backroom boy in a trap which
must have been set for another. Pallant was saying to Russell
quietly:

"We'll come last, if I may, to how Bullen got there since it leads
logically to a decision on action. For the moment there's the
immediate problem that it's bound to come out who Bullen was."

"It's lucky the duty officer kept his head."

"The D.O. did very well indeed. Bullen phoned in with the
address he was going to and asked for a check at his flat next
morning. When that produced no answer the D.O. acted. He
didn't collect a posse and rush there, he simply rang the police.
Who found Bullen. That gives us time to talk but not much more.
Bullen had his name in his jacket, something no outside man
would ever do, but even if he hadn't had it's inevitable he'll be
traced to us."

"When the fat will be in the fire."

"I'm afraid so. The responsible papers will play it down but
others will smell a story and run it. And we have very few friends
on the Left in parliament. There'll be a storm of questions which
will go to the P.M. who at the end of the line is responsible for
Security."

"Who can block them with the standard formula."

"I sincerely hope so," Pallant said. He wickedly mimicked the
Prime Minister's voice. " 'It is not in the national interest to
disclose ...' Just the same there'll be an ugly uproar and the
Executive will earn a large Black with its masters."

"What will you tell them?" Russell asked.

"The truth, the whole truth and nothing but. And hope that I
am believed though I may not be. I shall say that Bullen was acting

91

unauthorisedly and if asked for his motives I'll give a wrong guess at them."

"Good luck," Russell said. "I've been there myself."

"I've talked enough – your turn, I think. I'd like to hear you on the state of play generally."

"You think that would be useful?"

"Surely."

Charles Russell collected his thoughts deliberately; he had realised that he wouldn't be there if Pallant hadn't valued experience. "Then as I see it the stage now holds four players. The three principals are Abdel, Henshawe and Ahab, with Barbara Rhys-Harte in a minor role."

Willy Smith said quickly: "Not so minor. She was planted by Ahab to spy on Henshawe and has now returned to Ahab's bed."

"I didn't know that and it may be significant but we'll take it in my order if we may." It was the lightest of reproofs and not a snub. "So let's start with Abdel, by far the most powerful, and who hasn't yet put his hand on the table." Russell turned to Pallant. "You're shadowing him?"

"No, I am not."

Charles Russell accepted the brevity blandly since he both understood and entirely approved. It wasn't his diplomatic status which prevented Pallant putting a tail on him but the fact that Abdel would certainly notice it. Russell himself had had diplomats shadowed and to some odd assignations they'd led their shadows, but none of them had been both diplomat and head of a President's Private Bureau who had been through the mill and knew its workings. Abdel would spot a tail at once and promptly close down on whatever his plan might be. That would mean more and indefinite delay and the one thing which Pallant most lacked was time. Charles Russell nodded and Pallant went on.

"We know several things about Abdelaziz and several more we can safely assume. We *know* that his embassy has been smuggling in arms and that Henshawe was the man to distribute them. We know that because the late Maoui told us. Then Abdel appears in the cloak of a counsellor. It's quite possible he knocked off Maoui though it isn't in our book to try to prove it. So we go to where the arms are hidden but Henshawe gets there first and recovers them.

He will know where they went to and so will Abdel, because though we haven't been tailing Abdel himself we've done the usual things about Michael Henshawe, and we know the two have been in touch. The point is that neither will lead us to those arms." Pallant looked at Russell. "Now Henshawe."

"On what you tell me Henshawe's frozen. There's nothing he can do effectively without blowing where those arms are hidden. Did Anne Bullen persuade him to talk to Willy?"

"She did that."

"And what happened?"

Pallant waved at Willy who said: "I made him the orthodox proposition that, if he'd say where the arms were, we'd tell the police who would treat them as just another haul. But he wouldn't bite on that – why should he? He may not be a professional agent but he isn't the type to betray his paymaster. But he did give me one interesting snippet: he has heard of Ahab. He had heard of him through Barbara Rhys-Harte who I told him had been sent to spy on him. And Barbara Rhys-Harte was once friendly with Bullen."

Jack Pallant said: "I'm not sure I'm following."

"We're agreed that Bullen was not the real target?"

"Nobody could have known he would go."

"And the natural man to send would have been me. It's my case and I'm an active operator."

"Not an adequate reason to wish to kill you."

"I respectfully suggest it was."

"But why?"

Willy Smith said deliberately: "Because I'm black. I can go where whites can not and I sometimes do."

There was a minute while the other two thought. Finally Russell said softly: "Ahab." He turned again to Pallant. "What do you know?"

"He's done nothing illegal in England so far but we have reports on him from four different countries and none of them is reassuring. We also know that the ghettos are restive – Bristol proved that if proof were needed. I told you before I dislike the word 'cell' since it can mean anything from disgruntled layabouts to a cohesive and well-led group of effectives. But cells there almost certainly are, though we haven't proof that Ahab is organising them."

"In which case I must agree with Willy. Willy would be a real threat to Ahab."

There was another pause for thought, then Russell. "So the hypothesis, and that's all it is, is that somebody went to Bullen and set a trap. The bird expected was William Wilberforce Smith but Bullen went himself and got killed."

Jack Pallant nodded. "It does stand up."

"And the somebody?"

"That's a guess and for the moment irrelevant. I have made up my own mind but am not wasting time on her. Ahab is what matters now."

"That's what I said to Henshawe," Willy said.

"How did he take it?"

"Coolly enough, though I told him how I saw things as they stand. I told him that to the best of our knowledge Ahab had no arms whilst he had. So long as that situation continued he, Henshawe, was in increasing danger. But whatever Henshawe may be he's no quitter. Unfortunately he's also innocent — innocent in his new profession. So besides the men who shadow him I put on a couple of reliable guards."

"You did well," Pallant said; he went back to Russell. "So there for the moment it stands. But for one thing. To use that horrible word again, we ought to know much more about those cells. And I cannot see how we're going to do it. We can't send spies to six major cities even if we have the right men to handle it."

"You could pick on one," Willy said. "Guess the rest."

"All right. Which one?"

"The one in London under our noses. Something is brewing down in the Market."

"How do you know?"

"From my wife — she shops there. She's also a very observant woman. She doesn't have anything firm to go on but if she says there's a smell then smell there is."

"Then whom are we going to send?"

"Myself."

There was a second of almost total astonishment. Jack Pallant said: "But —"

"I'm as black as they are."

94

Pallant was close to losing his temper. "Of course you're black – I'm not yet blind. But you wouldn't have a hope in hell."

"I've done it before."

"I know you have. You've done it with your own sort of people. In the Market you'd be spotted at once. They aren't your sort of people by a mile."

"You are thinking of the way I speak?" Willy said it without embarrassment since he was neither proud of the way he spoke nor ashamed that other blacks spoke differently. "I agree that that is a disadvantage, but I think I can manage the rest quite easily. I can manage the woolly hat and the jeans, I can manage the bit about sticking my crutch out. I have a very strong beard and I don't need a big one. I thought perhaps a neat Imperial."

Jack Pallant said: "You're mad."

"Perhaps."

"In any case I'm not going to send you."

"Suppose I volunteer."

"That's different."

Charles Russell cut in at once. "It is not. In the army there was an admirable adage: never, but never refuse an order and never volunteer for anything." He stared at Pallant hard. "Up to you."

"You're putting me between the horns."

"Precisely where I intended to put you."

"You think I should give him an order?"

"Emphatically."

"Which one?"

"Not for me."

Pallant thought it over irritably; at last he said: "Very well, you can go."

"Not good enough," Russell said at once. "No permissive is a proper order."

Pallant looked at Charles Russell with open resentment. "Damn you," he said, "and damn the army. You're telling me how to run my business."

"I'm telling you that when I ran it I never accepted volunteers."

"Why not?"

"It's immoral."

The word released a growing tension for it wasn't one of

Russell's favourites. Jack Pallant began to smile and then laughed; he swung on Willy Smith and said formally:

"Go, Willy Smith. And the best of luck to you."

The elocutionist made a comfortable living by improving the speech of other West Indians who wished to advance their social class. He used the phrase freely and perfectly openly, since he wasn't a man to reject useful words for no better reason than that some people shrank from them. He operated from close to Harley Street. His fees were high but his clients could bear them. The people who came to 'learn to speak proper' had mostly succeeded in making money. Above all things he was entirely discreet. He had to be or lose his practice.

He was a little puzzled by Willy Smith. His appearance said money but not new money. His clothes were expensive but also quiet.

"How can I help you?"

"You can alter my speech."

"Say 'How now brown cow.' "

"How now brown cow."

The elocutionist was more puzzled than ever but he was honest as well as a good elocutionist. He wouldn't take fees for doing nothing. At last he said:

"I don't think I can help you, sir. You speak as well as I do or better."

"I think there must be some misunderstanding. I want my speech pulled down, not up."

The elocutionist didn't believe his ears. A barely possible explanation was that this elegant man had a girlfriend less so who was ribbing him over the way he spoke. Then why not bring her here and improve her? But he couldn't say that so said instead:

"How long have you spoken the way you do?"

"Ever since I went to prep school."

"How did your father speak?"

"Not too badly. He was second generation – I'm third."

The elocutionist shook his head unhappily. "It's going to be a very long job. It is not for me to ask your motives but you can't do it by just sticking 'Man' on your sentences."

96

"That I had rather assumed. And so?"

"Have you ever been an actor?"

"Never."

"Can you read phonetic script?"

"I can not."

The elocutionist drew a bow at a venture. "Three months," he said. "Three months at least."

"You can't cut that down?"

"I could but I wouldn't take the risk. You've got to be taken to pieces thoroughly. Do anything less and you'll just sound eccentric. You'll be neither fish nor fowl nor good red herring."

"I can't afford three months."

"I'm sorry. It would have been interesting to say the least."

"How much do I owe you, please?"

"Twenty guineas."

Amanda, his wife, was saying to Willy: "I wish you'd take that horrible beard off."

"If I did I'd have to wear a falsie and the Executive doesn't approve of disguises."

He realised he was inviting questions. He wasn't supposed to tell her his business but he couldn't strike her blind every evening, and at half-past eleven he had come home in strange clothing. He always took a bath before joining her.

"You need a disguise to go down to the Market?"

... So she knows that, does she? That makes it easier.

"How did you find that out?"

"I saw you. You were prowling about and I think you'd been smoking."

"Perfectly correct on both counts."

"As for the smoking, please be careful. As for the prowling about, it's your job. I've been doing a little myself in my amateur way."

"And what have you found?" He was eager for she was perspicacious.

"If I tell you you've got to tell me what *you've* got."

He hesitated, this was breaking the rules, but she was clever and she was also secure. Finally he nodded acceptance.

"You remember I once spoke of the Saviours? It was something I heard as men passed me talking. I remember you didn't think much of it at the time."

"And probably I was wrong. Go on."

"Well, I used the phrase myself as a try-on. I used it to the woman I buy chickens from. She went greyish and clammed up at once. Normally she'll natter all morning."

"Would you say she was frightened?"

"Scared to death."

"Anything else?"

"No, nothing concrete. But I'm sure there's something brewing up. On the surface it's all the same as it was but underneath there's trouble and plenty."

"Much my own impression," he said.

"All right. Your turn." She added as an afterthought: "I wonder you get a thing from anybody."

"You're thinking of the way I speak? I've a story for that."

"It must be a good one."

"I admit I come from a well-to-do family but I've revolted against their silly shams. I've reverted and I like it better. So I come to the Market for pot and women."

"I don't like the pot and I hate the women."

"You needn't worry I sleep with them but I talk to them in the pubs they drink in. Whores pick up more than most pro agents."

"You're growing up," Amanda said. "And what do these charming ladies tell you?"

"Like your chicken-woman I think they're frightened."

"Whores often are."

"But not of a beating. There's something more than that."

"Well what?"

"I think there's a cell in the Market."

"A cell?"

"Jack Pallant doesn't like the word either. What I mean is really an organisation, say a dozen men with a known objective, the fuse for the underlying dynamite."

"Was there a cell at Bristol?"

"We think so."

"Christ," she said. "Then it's really serious."

He had broken one rule and would bend another. In any case he entirely trusted her. "There may well be others in other cities."

"Never mind the other cities. We happen to live in London — three of us. How near is this explosion? You owe me that."

"You'd go away with the baby?"

"No. But get on with it."

"It's very hard to say how near. I'm convinced that there's a cell in the Market but my impression is that it's not a tight one. It couldn't be if it has to have frighteners."

"Frighteners?"

"To hold it together."

"Or," she said softly, "to frighten *you*."

"I've been taught to take care of myself."

"Against guns?"

"We don't think they have guns. Not yet."

He could see that she would have liked to cry but she wouldn't do so until she'd finished. "Have you told Pallant this?"

"Of course."

"How does he take it?"

"He takes it seriously."

"So," she said grimly, "so do I."

He had always known her mind worked fast but now she pinned the essential neatly. "If you've found out all this why go back to the Market?"

"I've told you too much already."

"A compliment."

He hesitated but he had gone too far. "We want the name of the man behind this cell."

"Surely you must suspect it?"

"We do."

"But you're going back for corroboration?"

"I must or throw my hand in. Resign."

He guessed that she was fighting temptation, to talk about herself and the baby, but she finally said in a very small voice:

"You mustn't do that — I wouldn't like it. When I married you I knew what you did."

"I think you're a very nice girl indeed."

"But if you get this man's name I think you're dead."

Later that night he woke alone. She was sitting in an armchair, weeping. He got out of bed and carried her back to it. "Don't worry, love. There's nothing to fret about. The Market is as tame as a henrun."

On Saturday evenings the Market split its seams, as much a social occasion as one for trade. It was crowded, earthy, good-tempered, free-spending. There appeared to be no shortage of money. Lights blazed from the shops and the stalls on the street, and from a record shop with an outside amplifier the latest group blared its jungle euphoria. Boys and girls were dancing to its beat, bouncing up and down like puppets, occasionally crying out like animals. The group drowned the background shouts of the stall-holders who shouted more from habit than need. They always did very well on Saturday nights. The older women wore fur coats when they had them, but apart from the biting English evening the scene could have been some minor carnival on an island under a mild tropical moon.

The uniformed policeman was patrolling his manor and the word was, for once, rather more than colloquial. He lived round the corner, he knew the people, and intelligent superiors had allowed him to stay where he was, a survival. He belonged to another age and climate, the world of the patronal village bobby. He never wore a flat hat on principle but he did wear two medals he'd earned in Ulster. Many men knew him and those that did liked him. If they must have a policeman walking these streets of theirs this was the sort of policeman they preferred. He knew perfectly well that stolen goods were handled on many stalls with impunity but these people seldom stole from each other. When they did it was his personal business but stealing somewhere else was not. Occasionally an older man greeted him.

"Good evening, copper."

"Good evening, dad."

So he paced these streets like a squire his acres but he was also quietly doing his job. Which was less to suppress a breach of the peace than to foresee one and, if he could, avert it. And two young men were behaving suspiciously. They were stopping at any stall which sold carpets, looking closely and then going away. The policeman thought it distinctly odd. A man might go shopping for carpets alone, though more likely he would bring his wife with him, or two women would be together for company. But two *men* buying carpets?

It didn't look right.

What the uniformed policeman feared was a snatch. The two young men were neatly dressed and one of them was wearing dark glasses. There was something about them vaguely professional. They went through the arch which pierced the brick viaduct, above them the loopline which by-passed the station. They turned right to where the Market began to thin. Here, on the right, in the viaduct's brickwork, were a shop or two and a few small warehouses, and on the other side of the street the stalls. The uniformed policeman followed discreetly.

The two young plainclothesmen were also uneasy for they were doing a job they thought was foolish. Every man in the Met knew this Market was crooked but provided it behaved with discretion – not jewellery, for instance, or something from Sotheby's – the policy was to turn a blind eye. And a perfectly sane and defensible policy. What fell off lorries went somewhere, sometime, and any organised drag might have met resentment. These people were known to be highly volatile and the politics must be considered too. There'd be immediate complaints of discrimination, an uproar about police brutality. Not many people would really believe it but those who did, or more likely pretended to, had the means to stir up a sea of trouble.

So these carpets were an unwelcome exception, the more so since again there was politics. The firm which had lost them had friends in high places, so high that they had been able to pester an already overloaded commander. So the word had gone out along with photographs, and the two young Jacks were obeying an order which they privately thought unwise, even reckless.

As they went past the shops in the wall of the viaduct one of them stopped the other. "Look." Outside an ironmonger's was an extensible ladder, its tip against the viaduct's parapet. "I need a ladder." He went inside.

When he came out he was clearly excited. "I could have it for three fivers," he said. "The normal price is round about forty."

"Don't risk it," the man in glasses said. "You could save yourself twenty-five quid and lose your job."

"I'm afraid you're right." But he sounded reluctant.

They had turned from the shop when Glasses stiffened. "Look at that stall over there without seeming to. The roll last but one on the right."

The other looked. "It's pretty like one of them."

"I suppose we'll have to check."

"I suppose so."

They walked to a street-light and looked at their photographs. "That's it all right."

"I wish it wasn't."

Behind the stall stood a man and a woman. The man was in his early thirties, bearded, broad-shouldered, his forearms bare. The woman was little more than a girl.

"May we look at that carpet, please?"

"I can't stop you." He'd been in trouble before and could smell a Jack.

They looked closely and nodded. It was a horrible artificial Wilton but it sold by the mile and had also been stolen.

"I must ask you to come to the station with me."

"Show me your warrant cards first."

They showed them.

The uniformed man had come up behind them and what he was seeing was much offending him . . . Jacks on his patch and without even telling him! It was little short of criminal trespass. But he wasn't going to interfere; he backed away to the wall and stood quietly aloof.

The man behind the stall made his break. He threw it over and jumped it cleanly, landing against the smaller Jack. He staggered and Glasses moved to catch him. The stall-holder was across the road and going up the ladder like an ape. At the top he climbed the parapet, standing on the track and mocking the Jacks. "Come and get me, you bastards."

He threw down the ladder. It fell in the street with a ringing crash.

The two plainclothesmen ran to pick it up but the uniformed man moved out of the shadows. He said in his fatherly way:

"I wouldn't do that."

"Why the hell not?" They were humiliated and therefore angry.

"Because it's a single line up there – a loop. What comes down it is mostly goods trains going fast. You wouldn't have a hope in a hundred."

The girl was screaming abuse hysterically and from nowhere a knot of men was growing. They were surly but they weren't yet menacing. The stall-holder was still mocking the Jacks.

The uniformed man went back to his wall. He knew in his bones what was going to happen. He had seen it once before and been helpless. He called to the Jacks:

"Get out of it while you can. Get out."

But they stood their ground and the constable listened. He could hear it in the distance, growing, the rumble of a freight train going fast. A man in the street had heard it too and he shouted to the stall-holder:

"Jump."

He didn't jump; he continued to taunt.

There was an urgent blare from the engine's siren, the scream of powerful brakes applied violently.

"Jump, for Christ's sake. Jump. Jump. Jump."

The stall-holder had begun to move but he'd been over-confident and had left it too late. There was a single despairing cry, then silence.

It was broken by the stall-holder's girl. "Murderers," she was screaming now. "Murderers, all of you. Bloody murderers."

The knot of men was now a crowd, growing fast as others ran up to join it. Three older men detached themselves quietly. One stood on each side of the uniformed constable and one stood in front to block all movement. They were less a menace than a protective barrier. In their nostrils was the scent of trouble and they didn't want a good cop injured. He said a little helplessly:

"You're obstructing an officer in the exercise of his duty." It sounded quite absurd and he knew it.

"Just keep quiet and we'll look after you."

For the first time in his life the policeman drew his stick on duty. Two of the three took it from him gently.

In the street there was the deadly moment when a crowd stood balanced between disturbance and riot. It broke as a man said: "Get them." He had a knife.

The Jacks had begun to move already but, like the stall-holder, they had left it too late. They had maybe five yards start but no more and a sea of what were suddenly savages was behind them with knives and smelling blood. They ran through the arch to the market proper and the roaring rout went through it after them. As it hit the main market the noise increased fourfold.

The constable said to the men who were blocking him: "You've got to let me go."

"Don't be dumb. What can you do against that lot? Nothing. If you want to be useful get on your radio."

The advice was sound and he pulled it out. "Scipio to Control –"

A tense voice said: "Cut it out. Talk fast."

"There's a disturbance in Pacific Street –"

The voice laughed harshly. "Is there indeed! The switchboard's jammed with reports of a riot."

Another voice came on, more authoritative. "Constable?"

"Sir."

"Where are you now?"

"In Pacific Street still."

"Then do not move from it. Don't try to earn another gong. We're getting men together as fast as we can. Do you hear me?"

"Yes sir."

The riot went raging across the market, throwing down stalls on both sides of the street, ripping off legs as immediate weapons. It was totally out of control, insensate.

The two Jacks had made a yard or two since the sheer size of the mob impeded its progress, but in front were two men who were running strongly. One had a razor and the other a cosh. Behind was the bass of angry men, pierced by the treble screams of women. There was also the acrid smell of burning. Some of the stalls had been lighted by pressure-lamps and these, when they'd been swept down by the torrent, had ignited the fabrics and plastics below them.

But the Jacks were not thinking of fires or of fire engines. They were thinking of saving their lives if they could. They were running with their heads down, panting, frightened and with very good reason. Their patrol car was still half a furlong distant and the two men behind them were closing fast.

Their driver had heard the uproar but kept his head. He had his engine running, the back door open. The two Jacks dived in and slammed the door. The man with the cosh threw his chest on the bonnet. He smashed the windscreen and jabbed at the driver. The driver moved his head and let in the clutch. The man with the cosh fell off in the road.

They drove perhaps a couple of miles before the driver said casually:

"Quite an evening."

It was Glasses who answered though he'd long since lost them. "And you know what we're going to get for it, don't you?"

The driver nodded; he too knew the form. "You're going to get a flaming rocket."

"It was lucky they didn't have guns or we shouldn't be here."

Chapter 9

The three young hoods were drinking beer, a beverage they disliked and despised. For one thing it made you pot-bellied and ugly and for another they'd grown accustomed to whisky. They had not been surprised when Ahab's money had stopped since they had killed a man when they'd been clearly told not to and moreover, though this wasn't their fault, they had realised they had killed the wrong man. Ahab had cut them off as he'd threatened to, refusing to see them or to answer their calls. None of them had steady employment or indeed the smallest chance of getting it, and such pennies as they scraped together came from pilfering and petty extortion. They were back on the scrapheap with hundreds of others. But they had grown used to Ahab's quite generous subventions and when the support was removed they had nothing to lean on. The eldest one finished his beer and said:

"We've got to get back."

"With Ahab?"

"Who else?"

"He won't even see us."

"He might if we brought him something worth buying."

The other two thought it over laboriously; they weren't very bright in the head and it took them some time. One said at length:

"But we know he's got men here as well as us three. Wouldn't they have told him already?"

"Not this bit, man."

"Why not?"

"They don't drink here."

"Then what have you got?"

The eldest of the three considered. He wasn't very good at explaining so he fed it them in single sentences.

"You know that Uncle Tom Nig who comes here?"

"The one who chats the tarts up?"

"That's him. He pretends to be a drop-out from some family with plenty of money."

107

"And isn't he?"

"I think he's a ferret. A police ferret or maybe something worse."

"Why shouldn't he be what he says – a drop-out."

"Because he doesn't behave like a drop-out. He drinks a good deal but I don't think he likes it and when he smokes grass he's pretty careful. That isn't drop-out form at all."

The other two worked it out again slowly. "Where does Ahab come into this?"

"For the tip-off. If there's somebody poking about he would want to know. If we're lucky he might even pay us."

The man who'd killed Bullen was far from intelligent but like most stupid men he had sudden flashes. "I've got it," he said triumphantly.

"What?"

"The man we were sent to rough up was going to be black. Ahab wanted him out of the way. He was dangerous because he'd been spying on Ahab. This drop-out is also black and spying."

The eldest hoodlum said: "Man! Oh man!" He thought the other offensively thick and his savage temper had landed them drinking beer. But he hadn't thought of this himself and he didn't conceal his admiration. "That's a winner," he said.

"So what'll you do?"

"I'm going to ring up Ahab now."

"Don't tell him the whole story."

"I'm not a fool."

He came back in five minutes, grinning happily. "We're to go to Ahab's pad in a cab."

Ahab had decided that he'd have to see them, though at the moment they were his unfavourite people. They had been told to put a black into hospital and instead they had casually killed a white. How the white had got there instead of the black was something which Ahab could only guess at: it was the killing which had made him furious. The Executive would not have been pleased if one of their men had been put out for a fortnight but that had been a fact he'd accepted. A killing was entirely different: the whole weight of a powerful machine would go into gear. It must be known that he was now in England, at the lowest an object of grave suspicion. In several countries where Ahab had worked he'd probably be in prison already and if it wasn't his other hand it would be a foot. That didn't happen here, or not yet, but a dangerous enemy had been unnecessarily provoked. Ahab still had plenty of money but he didn't have Henshawe's arms or unlimited time. And now such time as he had had probably lessened. He wasn't pleased with the men who had caused it but it was possible they had stumbled on something so he gave them chairs and prepared to listen.

"What's this about a spy in the Market?"

The eldest said: "What's it worth to us?" He had always been scared white of Ahab who, if he wished to, could pull his head off, but he wasn't going to talk for nothing.

"A hundred quid if the story stands up."

"We want our jobs back."

Ahab said coolly: "Don't be silly. If the story's a good one I'll make it two hundred."

"We're not talking without our jobs."

"Then get out."

The eldest looked at the other two miserably. They hesitated but finally nodded.

Ahab let him tell his story. Occasionally he asked a question when the sequence of events wasn't clear but generally he listened in silence. At the end he got up and went to his desk. He was a man who liked to know his enemies and he had a photograph of William Wilberforce Smith. He had been put to some trouble to get such a thing but a local photographer had kept the negative of the wedding group. Willy was wearing a morning coat and his cravat would not have disgraced Beau Brummell. Amanda was on his arm looking pleased. He put the photograph on the table.

"Well?"

Somebody said: "She's not very pretty."

"She doesn't have to be pretty, she's rather rich. So for that matter is the man she's marrying. Money marries money, you know." It was said without a hint of resentment. It was one of the facts of life, ineluctable. "Now what about the man?"

"Ours has a little beard."

"Which can be grown. Same sort of age and build?"

"Much the same."

"How does he talk?"

"He talks posh!"

"He would."

The eldest had been looking carefully. "It's him," he said at last. "I'd bet on it."

"Or kill on it? This time on orders."

There was a frozen silence.

"I thought you wanted your jobs back."

"We do."

Ahab had made his mind up instantly . . . Two men or one – now it wasn't significant. The Executive would be angrier than ever, but the heat was bound to be turned on him sometime and he couldn't afford a spy in the Market. It wasn't secure and on the least hint of hard evidence . . .

He simply couldn't afford the time.

"When will you see this man again?"

"He comes down most nights."

"Then do it tonight."

"That doesn't give us much time to plan."

"Plan what? It's dark outside when the pubs shut, isn't it?"

The eldest looked again at the other two. One of them said: "We can try."

"Do that. Gentlemen, you have your jobs back."

Amanda wasn't often bitchy but tonight she was putting the knife in hard. "When are you going to stop this Market lark?"

"Give it a day or two more."

"Why should I? I hate that beard and you've started to smell."

He could see she was tense and played her cool. "I take a bath every evening before I come near you."

"I know you do and it doesn't work."

"So what have I started to smell of?"

"Them."

"Aren't you being a little snobbish, dear?"

She blew up in a magnificent temper. "So snobbish, am I? And what about you? Those clothes you pay a fortune for, that hideous old school tie, the cricket –"

"I used to be quite good at it once."

"Meaning before you married me?"

He knew she was bent on a row and he was tired. Normally he mildly relished a tiff, it added salt to a successful marriage, but tonight he said:

"Come clean, love. What's eating you?"

"I told you. That bloody Market."

"What of it?"

"You know there was a riot there yesterday."

"It didn't come near the pub I was sitting in."

"And there's another thing you've started to smell of."

"I gargle –" he began.

"So if I were you I'd watch the pot."

"All in the line of duty."

"Balls. And what do you hope to get out of it?"

"Just a name."

"And if you get it what are you going to do?"

He said soberly: "We're not the police."

She was instantly as quiet as he was, a woman fearing for her man and showing it. "You mean you might take your own sort of action?"

"I think I've said too much."

"Too little. I've guessed you sometimes play dangerous games. Hasn't it occurred to you that your enemies can play them too?"

"I take money for knowing exactly that."

"Come into the bedroom," she said. He was surprised for they had still been eating but he followed her to the bedroom obediently. She looked at the cot where the baby was sleeping. He was full of what he liked most and flat out. His sleep was almost a conscious act.

"Look at him," Amanda said.

"He looks fine to me."

"Of course he's fine – I'm a pretty good mother. But he wouldn't be half as fine without a dad."

"That's blackmail," he said.

"Choose your own bloody word."

Unexpectedly she began to weep and she didn't cry pointlessly, she wasn't the type. He put an arm round her waist and led her

111

back to the dining room. There was food on the table still but both ignored it. They sat on the sofa holding hands till she wiped her streaming face.

"I'm sorry."

"May it do you good."

"You're a prince."

"In that pub in the Market they think I'm a drop-out."

"You're sure of that?"

"If they don't I'm in trouble."

"How many times are you going back?"

"Two," he said vaguely. "Two or three."

"Will you compromise?"

"I might for you."

"Make tomorrow the last time."

"All right."

It didn't distress his conscience to say it. Unknowingly he thought as had Ahab ... Two days or one – it wasn't significant. He knew that he was getting nowhere.

In the night he heard her mutter and then sit up. "What's the matter, love?"

"I had a dream."

It wasn't true, she had thought of a proverb, and saws often enshrined an ancient wisdom. He had promised to go just once more ...

Just so. And the saw had said to her "Last Time Unlucky."

The three young hard men were back on the whisky but drinking with an unusual restraint. It was going to be a working evening. When Willy came in he sat down at the bar and they moved from their table to either side of him. Willy had often bought them drinks but tonight the eldest said:

"What's yours?"

"A small whisky, please."

The other ordered a double and passed it to Willy, paying from a considerable roll. All three of them wore leather jackets and Willy noticed that they'd been recently cleaned. They must have pulled off some minor coup, probably a straightforward mugging. And he noticed another thing too: they drank slowly. On other

112

occasions when he had seen them in funds they had drunk too much and done it too fast but this evening they were making them last.

"Have another drink?"

"Not yet, thanks."

The eldest re-ordered nevertheless and Willy poured even more water than usual. Two girls came in and he moved to join them. He didn't suppose he'd get anything new but he preferred them to the three young hoods who had an air of purpose he hadn't seen. One of them put a hand on his shoulder.

"Not tonight, my friend – we're the hosts tonight. You've bought us a lot of rounds and we're buying some back." He added with an open contempt. "And anyway you never go home with them."

When the pub shut they all four went out together. It was a shabby pub in what was almost a slum, half a mile from the Market's cheerful lighting. The street had lamps but most had been vandalised. This was where the girls lived, some well. At the end of it Willy had parked his car. It was a hired car – he always used one on night jobs.

Willy knew with a sudden animal instinct that he must reach it or he was going to die.

The other drinkers had come out too but there hadn't been many and they thinned away quickly. Willy started to walk down the empty street. The three were fifteen yards behind him.

He had drunk more than he wished but his head was clearing. They would jump him when he reached the car. He would need to unlock it, get in, start the engine ...

Fifteen yards wasn't nearly enough. His only chance to increase it was to run. He started to do so and the hard men ran too.

Willy knew after thirty yards that he'd made a mistake. Normally he was fit and fast but whisky had upset his stomach and too much pot had cut his wind. He had done his course in unarmed combat, he would have faced a single cosh or razor, and the men behind were as unfit as himself. True. But they were also three. Sooner or later they'd pull him down by sheer weight, literally get him down on the pavement, and there they would cut him to ribbons or kick him to death. He had a crippling stitch, his pace

113

was slowing. His breath was coming in ragged gasps.

The door of a house beside him opened and a girl stood on the steps in her warpaint. When she saw running men she started to shut it but Willy ran up the steps and bundled her back. He shut and bolted the door behind him. "Fifty quid for the night," he said.

At the local rates it was overgenerous.

The girl hesitated, said finally: "Show me."

Willy never went out unprepared for emergencies and he gave her five tenners which she put in her bosom. She was a big buxom girl and not bad looking.

Outside in the street the three men had stopped. One of them said:

"She'll have a telephone – most of them do."

"That's right."

"So if we try to break in she'll ring the police and if we wait for him he'll ring his own people."

"Right again. So what do we do? Ahab is going to give us hell."

The eldest considered and finally spoke. "We've got to get out of here – on the run. Ahab gave us a float and there's still a bit left."

"Where are we going to go?"

"Who cares? Birmingham, Leicester, Bristol – toss for it. Anywhere but back to the Market."

"And how are we going to live when the float's gone?"

"Try and find another Ahab."

"Not much chance of that."

"I know."

Inside the flat Willy Smith was recovering. The girl asked softly: "Trouble?"

He nodded. "You could truthfully say I was deep in trouble."

"Where did you learn to talk like that?"

"At school. And now if I may use your telephone?"

She was at once suspicious. "Are you a copper?"

"I can promise you I'm not a policeman."

"Then who do you want to ring?"

"My wife."

She gave a big girl's deep contralto laugh. "Jesus, you've got a nerve," she said.

"You misunderstand me. Come along too and listen."

She sat beside him as he used the telephone. "Is that you Mandy?"

A worried voice said. "What's happened? It's late."

"There's been a bit of silly nonsense."

"Are you all right?" Amanda was even more worried now.

"Perfectly, thank you." He was still a little cross with her for the previous night she'd been bent on a row and he hadn't been in the mood to accept one. "I'm spending the night with a tart," he said.

"Then you needn't come back." It had been delivered with the crack of a pistol.

Again he said: "You misunderstand me, dear. The lady has been very helpful but I'm spending the rest of the night in a chair."

"But –"

"I'll tell you the whole story tomorrow."

Willy rang off.

The girl said: "Man, you're cool." She looked at him reflectively. He was dressed like a drop-out but clearly wasn't. "You're sure you meant that bit about a chair?"

"And a blanket if you have one, please."

"Fifty quid is a lot for a chair and a blanket."

"And another fifty tomorrow."

"Man!" Something of her earlier doubt returned to her. "You're sure you're not a copper?"

"I promised."

"You haven't come here to set me up?" It had happened once before when a busybody had caught her off guard.

"If you'd been outside you wouldn't ask it."

"All right," she said, "but I'll give you breakfast. What would you like?"

"Two eggs, please. Done lightly."

"It isn't a lot for a hundred quid."

"Which isn't a lot for saving my life."

115

Chapter 10

When Henshawe had taken a chance on the telephone Abdelaziz had said he would have to think, and being a deliberate man he had done so with deliberation. He had been sent to London on his father's mad plan (he was allowing the adjective now, though privately) and in the tangle of events which had followed he had decided that two threads were dominant. Henshawe had not been the man for the job and Ahab had emerged as a rival. Henshawe had no organisation, at the best only vague connections and sympathisers, whereas it looked a very good bet that Ahab had men in several cities who'd be prepared to use arms if they ever received them. Abdel knew who was sending money to Ahab, that international nuisance his neighbour, but so far he hadn't sent him arms. But his father had sent weapons before Henshawe could use them and that had been premature, a folly. It was unthinkable to let them fall to Ahab.

Abdel began to stalk the room. With his dressing gown and close-cropped head he looked like a monk in some silent cloister. It had been one thing to obey his father whatever increasing doubt had dogged him; he was a feudal man and in no way ashamed of it; but it would be something else entirely different, something eternally unforgivable, to arm a creature of his father's enemy.

From this reflection there emerged one certainty: he had to get those arms to safety, to where Ahab couldn't extort them from Henshawe. The simplest solution would be to call on the Executive who would then collect and be properly grateful, but whilst his father lived he couldn't do it – not the grossest betrayal of all his instincts. And Henshawe himself was certainly shadowed. If he went anywhere near those arms he'd blow them.

Another betrayal at one remove. He'd have to do it himself and he couldn't think how.

He took a very hot bath; he was cold and miserable; and on top of his problems he was lonely and homesick. He thought of his flat in his country's capital. It was small and spare for it wasn't his home.

His family rarely came to it, preferring a life in their native hills. His eldest son ran the land efficiently and Abdel flew there every week-end. It was simple and more than a little austere but it was what he loved best and he wouldn't change it.

And the loneliness was another factor, for notwithstanding four years at an English school England was an alien culture. The staff of the embassy knew who he was and mostly kept a respectful distance, and in any case he didn't much care for them. He had no friends from his four years learning English. The only man he cared for in England was one to whom he sent cards at Christmas, but one couldn't arrive at Charles Russell's door with nothing better than a sort of apology ... "My name is Abdelaziz. We haven't met for thirty-five years but I'd like to come in for a professional chat."

Besides being very doubtful manners, that would also be a gross impertinence. Abdel was head of the Private Bureau but the Private Bureau was not the Executive. Charles Russell had scalps at his belt which Abdel had not. Abdel had always admired him greatly and sometimes he had solved a problem by asking himself how Charles Russell would deal with it.

Such as getting those weapons away to safety.

It came to him in a blinding flash, as though Russell were present and sagely advising. Henshawe couldn't move the arms because Henshawe was being closely tailed. A blind brick wall? Not at all – an opening. Henshawe should be the decoy, taking nothing, while Abdel, the shadow drawn away, took the weapons. It would take a couple of days to arrange but it was the sort of outrageous plan which often came off.

Michael Henshawe had been telling himself that James Bullen's death was not his business, certainly not his responsibility, but Anne Bullen had told him that he worked in the Executive and he himself had been called there urgently. In that sort of world there were no coincidences and he would have admitted that he had liked Anne Bullen.

He shrugged since 'liked' was a gutless word. He considered again and finally rang her.

"I was sorry to hear of your brother's death."

"How did you know?"

"I read a newspaper."

"It didn't say whom he worked for?" She sounded anxious.

"No, but you told me."

"And you haven't told anyone else?"

"Why should I?" This conversation was not the one he'd expected.

"No news-hawks round your door?"

"Not one."

There was a pause, then she said in a different voice: "I'm afraid I've been distinctly rude. It will have to come out in the end of course, but they'd like to keep it quiet for a bit. But it was kind of you to ring."

"Not at all."

There was another pause, then the original voice again. "I'd like to talk to you."

"So would I."

"Could you come now?"

"I could. And with pleasure."

He had taken seriously Willy's warning of danger and the knowledge of it had sharpened his senses. In the Tube he thought he had spotted his shadow. He was a muscular man in a tartan muffler and was wearing pince-nez which looked wholly ridiculous. On an impulse Henshawe got up and spoke to him. If he happened to be wrong he'd be snubbed but that was a risk which he'd have to run.

"Am I right in thinking your job is to follow me?"

The man looked surprised but recovered quickly. If he'd been spotted that was a disadvantage but he could be easily changed if that were necessary. He laughed pleasantly and said:

"It is not. What I am is your block."

"My what?"

"I beg your pardon – a term of the trade. I am here to protect you from molestation."

The shadow was in fact a woman, sitting five seats away and reading a magazine. Muffler noticed that Michael Henshawe was staring. "You'll know me again but I can guess what's puzzling you. You're wondering about my pince-nez. You needn't. The

119

reason for them is perfectly logical. If you get into a fight they fall off. You don't have to waste time *taking* them off. The least violent movement and down they go."

"You are expecting violence?"

"I very much hope not."

"I'm grateful for your services – genuinely. I'm calling on a lady called Bullen."

"I've heard of her," the block admitted.

"I'll be getting out at Queensway."

"Then so shall I."

"Perhaps we could walk together?"

"Why not? I'd be very glad of exercise and also of agreeable company. As often as not on this job it's unpleasant."

At Anne Bullen's flat the block stayed outside and she let Henshawe in when he called on the intercom. He looked round the room in recognition for it was furnished with the sort of pieces which came from ancient country houses before designedly disruptive tax beat them into their native soil for ever.

He had begun again on condolences but she waved them aside with a sharp impatience. "It was a terrible shock and I haven't recovered, but there's nothing in the world I can do. The Executive won't admit whom he worked for till the first heat is off and they think they can ride it. No, I wanted to talk about you, not James."

"You flatter me."

"I'm sincerely interested."

She had given him a chair and a drink and he sat there at ease but also wary. She had told him she was a persuader once and it was certain she could be extremely persuasive. Finally she said:

"You're a fool."

"You're entitled to an opinion."

"Phooey! Don't try to ride me off. I'm a woman."

"So I observe."

"That bit might come later. For the moment you're in a trade you're not trained for."

"I'm beginning to think the same myself."

"Also you're in growing danger."

"So I was told at the Security Executive. Did you know that one

120

of their guards is outside this house?"

"No, I didn't know that but it doesn't surprise me." She leant forward suddenly. "I'm going to be rude again. When the Executive sends me out on a job it always gives me a background briefing. I know most things about you and some seem foolish."

"Go on," he said.

"You were chucked out of Sandhurst."

"For being clumsy at drill."

"Absurd of course, but hardly final. Then you go into a bank and pilfer." She held up a hand as he started to speak. "I know all about that business too. I know that there were other cases where nothing worse happened than instant dismissal and I know that they pursued yours relentlessly – set you up as the awful example to others. I'll admit that that was indifferent luck."

"It made me very bitter."

"No doubt. So off you go to a foreign country, one living in another century, and there you meet a rather splendid old man who also has reason to hate the English. He hires you for some preposterous plan, or preposterous without experienced agents."

"I told you I was as bitter as hell."

"It isn't that I mind – I've been bitter myself. My father married me off to a drunken old laird. No, I don't mind the chip on the shoulder at all. It isn't that which destroys you for me."

"Then what?"

"Your self-pity."

She could see that she had shaken him but also that she had made an impression. The shaft had gone home and the barb had bitten. He said at last:

"D'you know, I'd never thought of that."

"Do me a personal favour and think of it."

When Henshawe had gone she heard the telephone. She picked it up and a voice said:

"Miss Bullen?"

"Why, Willy Smith." The 'Miss Bullen' hadn't greatly surprised her. William Wilberforce Smith was a punctilious creature who had never been asked to call her Anne. He would therefore continue to call her Miss Bullen until he was invited to change. "What is it?"

"Is Michael Henshawe with you still?"

"He's just left. And if I'm not prying, how did you know?"

"We've a guard on him outside in the street."

"So Michael told me."

"He spotted him, did he? It doesn't matter."

She said on a note of open anxiety: "Willy, what's cooking?"

"I wish I knew."

"But you've got him covered?"

"We're doing our best."

She was suddenly furious. "Willy, don't cheat on me."

He was surprised but said mildly: "I don't think I'm cheating. I'm telling you we've got him covered but you know as well as I do that things can go wrong."

"I'll kill you if they do," she said.

Barbara Rhys-Harte had had another bad day. The case had been festering since the previous Christmas and FAAR was involved as a last resort. A post office in northern London had taken on extra staff for the extra mail and one of them had been a black. Since the man had been only barely literate there'd been a great many cases of misdelivery and many complaints which had been duly passed on. This, Barbara thought, was discrimination: special allowance should have been made for his handicap. And there the squalid affair might have ended if the man had accepted correction normally. But he hadn't accepted correction normally: instead he had turned bloody-minded. He'd gone out on his walk one day with the mail which he'd dumped in a municipal dustbin.

Unfortunately he had been seen to do so by respectable and unshakeable witnesses. Tampering with Her Majesty's Mail was something which could not be ignored and a conviction had followed, the sentence suspended.

And at once the bleeding hearts had sprung to arms. Money had been raised for an appeal. It had failed. There'd been a reference to a strange tribunal which could hold that a man had been sacked improperly. It had made the sympathetic noises which were basically what it was paid to emit but had been unable to hold that dismissal had been unreasonable. So here the case was on Barbara's desk. What particularly riled her was the reference to

Her Majesty's Mail. Any mention of royalty raised her hackles. Why, if the man had been on a paper round the matter would have attracted no interest. Evidently he'd been savagely victimised.

She would have liked to take the case to Ahab but she knew that he was privately stretched. The bishop of Crondal was in some African stateling on a crusade which would have no impact whatever and Lord Welcome-Wills was away on a holiday, in fact on one of his regular dry-outs. That left only Mrs Alderney Cohn, and Barbara doubted whether she carried the weight for a case which, though clearly a social scandal, was legally open and shut and forgotten. Nevertheless she sent her the papers.

She had doubted that Mrs Cohn had the weight but she hadn't expected an open snub. Mrs Alderney Cohn sent for Barbara Rhys-Harte, left her standing, and tapped the papers firmly.

"We can't interfere in this," she said.

"Why ever not?"

"Because," Mrs Alderney Cohn said carefully, "because those letters may well have held money. Postal orders perhaps, or cheques. Even dividends."

Barbara had flounced out in a huff. Rich old bitch, she had thought – she's not really with us.

She went home that evening in a very bad temper, cheered only by knowing that Ahab would meet her. He had a key to her flat but seldom went there for, secretly, her pad annoyed him. It had wall-to-wall carpeting which matched the striped paper, pictures of flowers by semi-professionals, china artefacts of no great distinction, and a good many family photographs in silver frames. It was the taste of a dimly dated suburbia and Ahab knew Barbara wasn't suburban. She was already rather more than well off and one day would be a wealthy woman. Wealth had its own queer obligations – not charity or good works, they were patronage – but matters like having good taste and indulging it. His own was for fine old colonial furniture, not this ragbag of expensive rubbish. The room offended Ahab deeply.

He wondered what she would do when FAAR collapsed. He was in a position to know that that was inevitable since he saw the accounts and they grew steadily worse. Despite the 'Foundation' there was no basic trust: the money was collected piecemeal and such as came in was decreasing alarmingly. The hundred pound donors were now down to ten, the small givers were coming up with nothing. Mrs Alderney Cohn was a very rich woman but she was too worldly to patch a sinking ship. Whilst FAAR could give her the chance to make mischief, the chance of the sort of prestige she valued, she would serve on its board and pay something to do so, but the moment the building began to subside she would move to another without a pang.

So what would Barbara Rhys-Harte do then? Ahab wasn't a man who laughed alone but now he gave a grunt of amusement. She wouldn't try for another FAAR since basically she was quietly conformist. When she'd worked off her absurd sense of guilt she'd go back to an ordinary life and enjoy it; she would go home and marry a gentleman farmer whom she'd educate to his great advantage. When I'm in prison, he thought, or more likely dead, she'll be giving the vicar tea and muffins.

She came in and gave him a gin and tonic. He had seen that there was drink in the sideboard in cut glass decanters which he had noticed weren't good ones, but he hadn't considered helping himself. She was beholden to him, very close to release, and he didn't wish to make it mutual even though in so small a matter as taking a drink she would not have begrudged him. When she'd come to him first he'd been rough and abrasive, he had wanted to take this randy Miss down, but by now he had grown quite fond of her, if not as a woman as a sort of case history. Her doctor, she had called him once, and he wasn't displeased he'd been able to help her.

He saw she was upset and edgy and asked at once: "Did you have a bad day?"

"That bloody Mrs Alderney Cohn."

"She's a bitch," he said with decision. "Forget her."

He didn't wish to discuss Mrs Alderney Cohn. He had formed his own opinion of her and if Barbara was coming round to it that wasn't in any way surprising. He shut his mind to her account of the morning but something she said at the end broke through.

"What's more I think she suspects what you really are."

He was instantly attentive. "Why?"

"Nothing definite. The way she looks at you."

124

"Nothing more than that?"

"Just a hunch."

He slowly relaxed – the girl knew nothing – but for a second she had severely shaken him. For at this of all moments he couldn't afford it, not a complication with Mrs Alderney Cohn. He was now at the edge of success or failure, and one thing essential had run rather well.

William Wilberforce Smith might not be dead but his cover had been blown wide open. He wouldn't be going again to the Market.

But everything else had run very badly. He had twice asked his patron to send him arms and twice his patron had answered evasively ... How big were his cells, were they ready, effective? And Ahab knew now that he couldn't wait long. The luck was running against him strongly; he had to have arms quickly or never.

... Michael Henshawe's arms or none at all. Ahab had a plan for that. He would try the proven methods first, like the taxi routine which often succeeded.

He considered what Henshawe might really hold – what sort of arms and how many of them. There'd be machine pistols and of course grenades, mines against tanks and APCs, perhaps even a hand-discharged missile or two. Certainly enough for the Market. It wasn't his best cell but it was surely his biggest and in any case, he must forget the others. There wasn't time, now, for coordination. And two nights ago the Market had rioted. If there'd been men in that riot bearing firearms and using them it wouldn't have been another Bristol; it would have been another Miami or worse.

Barbara was still talking resentfully but he interrupted with a sudden question. He had asked it before when less important but now the answer was an essential tool.

"What sort of man is Michael Henshawe?"

"He's gentler in bed than you were at first."

He thought her obsessed but didn't say so. "I didn't mean bed. I meant as a person."

She had been irritated by the switch of subject but could see he was putting the question seriously. "He's got a chip on his shoulder the size of a saucepan. He isn't driven like you – he's not quite so helpless – but you won't get whatever you want by just asking."

"Would money tempt him?"

"Never in this life."

"Then I'll have to think of something else."

"I can see that you already have."

Later he used the telephone and a woman's voice answered. "He's been located. He has gone to a woman's flat but she isn't a whore. He'll be out before the morning."

"Everything else in order?"

The voice was now offended. "It is. You paid our fee which isn't cheap. It isn't cheap because we're good. We'll ring you at the number you gave us the moment we have the goods for collection."

Barbara went to bed but Ahab sat on. He was hopeful but he mistrusted hope . . . *Hope is the father of all illusion.* He had read that in some Sufi poem. He didn't often read poetry and very seldom the mystics. All mystics were all the same – escapists.

And come to that, he thought, I'm one myself. I haven't really a hope in hell.

The guard outside Anne Bullen's house was radio-ing to William Wilberforce Smith. "It looks like the old taxi trick. There's one up the road and it's been there some time. Flag down. This isn't a street where drivers take time off."

"Colour of driver?"

"Indisputably white."

"That comes later if it comes at all. For the moment we're concerned with Henshawe. And, incidentally, myself as well."

"Why yourself?"

"I've been threatened with death if the job goes wrong. Do you want to know by whom?"

"I do not. But you could say I was on double duty."

"You can put it that way if you like."

"I like. I'm going to claim for double money."

"I always thought you had Greek blood somewhere."

Michael Henshawe went down the stairs of the flats, opening the hall door to the street. A taxi began to move towards him, putting up its flag as it came on. It had started to rain and he was grateful to see it. He gave the driver his address and opened the door.

A man came from nowhere and put a hand on his shoulder. Tartan muffler said firmly:

"Not that one, sir." He stepped back a pace, drawing Henshawe with him. The driver had begun to get down.

Muffler said to him coolly: "I wouldn't try that one, I really wouldn't."

The driver snarled. He was holding a razor. The guard let him raise it to slash, then moved. There was a scream of unexpected pain and the razor fell in the street with a clatter. So did the guard's absurd pince-nez. They had broken but he produced another pair. The driver was standing with one arm dangling.

"You'll have to drive one-handed, won't you?"

The driver got back in his cab with a groan. He fumbled with the gears but moved away.

Michael Henshawe said a little uncertainly: "So he was going to cut me up."

"Oh no. That was his own and private weapon and was probably against his orders. The real idea was a straightforward snatch. If you'd got into that cab you'd have had it. The driver could have locked the doors on you and somewhere along his route he'd have stopped. So another man gets in and there you are. Or another way, a bit more sophisticated, is to turn on some form of knock-out gas. In either case you'd come to somewhere strange and I'd guess that what happened thereafter would not be nice." The guard looked at Henshawe. "You look a bit shaken."

Henshawe didn't answer him. He had moved to a railing and was leaning against it. He would have faced a cosh or a gun with credit, but he wasn't a South American, he wasn't a Glaswegian gangster, and the razor had made him feel physically sick.

The guard echoed Anne Bullen's comment earlier. "Without impertinence, sir, you're in a trade you're not used to. And now, if I may, I'll see you home. We shan't get another taxi in these parts. Can you make it to the station?"

"Give me five minutes."

"A problem," the guard said reflectively. "Yes. They won't try

127

again with that taxi routine but they may have had a second string in case the taxi trick didn't work or went wrong, and standing still in a deserted street we're vulnerable to the crudest mayhem. They won't attack me alone – why should they? – but you're still a very tempting target." A thought struck him and he went on levelly. "Do you know the lady you've been with well?"

"Not very well."

"A pity, that. I was wondering whether she'd take you in. For an hour or so, I mean, till you're right again."

"I couldn't ask that."

"Perhaps not. But I could." The guard walked to the door and rang a bell. Anne's voice in the speaker said: "Who's there?"

"I believe I once had the pleasure of meeting you. In any case I'm the block on Henshawe. I'm sorry to say there's been an accident." He gave the outline of it, quick and succinct.

"Is he all right?" The voice was anxious.

"He's not injured but he's shaken up."

"What do you want me to do?"

"Take him in for a bit."

"Then send him up at once."

"And he needs a drink."

Henshawe had joined the guard by the bell. The latch clicked open, the door swung inwards. The guard pushed Henshawe through it firmly.

He went back to the street and radio-ed Willy. "It was a taxi-snatch as we thought."

"Which I trust you stopped."

"I stopped him from getting in all right but thereafter it didn't run quite to form. The driver got down and waved a razor. I had to do things and the affair shook Henshawe."

"Where is he now?"

"He's gone back to Miss Bullen for rest and refreshment."

"When are you due for relief?"

"In two hours."

"Would you care to bet?"

"It depends on what."

"That Henshawe won't appear till the morning."

"I never bet when I don't know the track form."

128

Anne Bullen put Henshawe on a rather small sofa with a brandy which he accepted gratefully. He wasn't trembling but was the colour of clay.

... If he starts to explain, to excuse himself, I never want to see him again.

What he did was the opposite; he took a long pull at the brandy and said: "The army was perfectly right to throw me out. Not because of the drill of course, but because I'd never have made a soldier."

Nothing he could have said would have pleased her more. The block had been brief but also explicit and she didn't think Michael Henshawe had been shamed. She didn't suppose he'd seen a razor before, a hideous weapon to face the first time, and on top of that had been sudden knowledge that in a hour or two, and probably less he'd be a whimpering pulp on some concrete floor. To take that in your normal stride, unshaken, you needed what Henshawe had not – experience.

And there hadn't been a hint of self-pity.

She could see that he was recovering fast and she hoped that he wouldn't spoil it all by offering any form of apology. Instead he finished the brandy and stood up. "You've been extremely kind,"he said formally. "Do you think that guard's outside still?"

She looked from the window. "He's there all right."

"In that case I'll join him."

"You can't do that."

"Why ever not?"

"You look all right but your head isn't functioning. They won't go for him alone –"

"He told me that."

"– but if you join him you put him at risk besides yourself. I know he's paid for what he does but I don't think you should presume on that."

"Presume," he repeated. The word had shocked him. He was a considerate man and had failed to consider. Finally he said uncertainly:

"But I can't stay here till it's light."

"Why not?"

129

She saw him look at the sofa and hid a smile. He was quite a big man and the sofa small.

"You'll find the bed a lot more comfortable."

Chapter 11

Abdel had had his illumination and was making his simple plan accordingly for his profession had taught him that simple was good. He had realised that he would need active aid, and his first thought had been a demand to his deputy to send suitable men to England immediately. But he had quickly decided that this was unnecessary. His embassy had a list of the students whom his country maintained to study in London and he picked from it four names of his own close clan. They might well not be the cleverest students but he could trust them as he could trust his own sons.

They stood before him now, respectfully silent.

"Good morning, gentlemen."

"Good morning, uncle." He wasn't their uncle but was related and older. 'Uncle' was therefore correct address.

He looked at them approvingly. They were stocky and powerful with the hillman's broad shoulders and wiry legs. He led them to the ambassador's study. Since Maoui's death it had not been used for the *chargé* had his own room and preferred it. The ambassador's study was dusty and stuffy, overcrowded with elaborate French furniture. Abdel waved a hand round the depressing room.

"How long to clear all that rubbish away?"

"Clear it to where, please?"

"Outside to a van."

They talked amongst themselves but quietly. They were in the presence of a respected elder and it wouldn't have been polite to raise a voice. Finally one said:

"Four hours."

Abdel was surprised. "As long as that?"

"It's pretty delicate stuff, you see. We couldn't go throwing it about like crates."

"Suppose it *was* crates?"

"Oh, that would be different. May I ask how many?"

"Twenty-three. Some are roughly the size of coffins, others of an old-fashioned tea chest."

"And you say we needn't handle them gently?"

"Not as gently as this furniture – no. But you can't go throwing them round like confetti. Some of them contain explosives."

None of the four faces moved. The students chatted again, then one of them said:

"In that case about an hour and a half."

"Excellent. Now listen carefully. You will come to my flat tonight at midnight. I have hired a self-drive removal van and in it we will drive to south London. There we will load those crates and drive off again. You needn't know our destination but at it we shall unload and drive home. Are there any questions?"

There were none. It would have been an insult to offer money and Abdel did not.

He then rang Michael Henshawe briskly. "Please come to my flat at once."

"Not to the Goat? You know I'm tailed."

"I know perfectly well you're being tailed." There was more than a hint of irritation, a grandmother being taught to suck eggs. "Your line is probably tapped as well and for all I know your flat is bugged. Mine isn't. So come to me."

Abdel kept whisky for foreign guests; he gave Henshawe a stiff one but not too stiff; he told him what he had told the students.

"You won't get away with that," Henshawe said.

"I shall with your cooperation."

"Then how do I cooperate?"

"Thus. You too have a van and two friends to drive it. It should call at your flat at twenty minutes past midnight. You will join it and drive away at once. Naturally not to where the arms are. Your tails are certain to have a car and are equally certain to use it to follow you. When they've gone I will collect the arms. You, in short, are the decoy for me. I shall take the arms and hide them safely until something happens to neutralise Ahab."

"Who had a go at me last night, by the way."

"What sort of a go?"

"The snatch by sham taxi."

"You spotted it?"

"No, but my guard did. He was very efficient."

132

"I believe you. The Executive doesn't use second-class men."
Abdel considered, then said almost casually: "I suppose you
realise he'll try again."

"He's as desperate as that?"

"For those weapons? I'm sure of it. And the only way he can find
them is through you."

"Not an engaging prospect."

"No. If I were you I'd hole up for a bit. Have you a safe house?"

"Perhaps ... Yes, I think so."

"Then I'd go to it as soon as you can. But not tonight – I need
your services."

"May I ask two questions?"

"I may not answer."

"Then where are you going to take those guns?"

Abdelaziz, unsmiling, told him.

"It's corny," Michael Henshawe said.

"Of course it's corn but corn mostly works. More accurately it's
a criminal cliché. Like the one about the fence and the diamonds.
The police come round with a warrant and search; they give it the
works and tear up the floorboards. But they don't find the
diamonds – they're round the wife's neck. And the second
question, please."

"When I'm out on the decoy run where do I go?"

"Drive anywhere but west of London. That's where I'm going
myself with the hardware."

Charles Russell was giving Jack Pallant dinner and it wasn't a meal
to which he'd looked forward. Jack Pallant had a troublesome
ulcer and at the moment it was playing him up. He had asked for
boiled chicken and milk as his beverage. Charles Russell detested
boiled chicken heartily but he could eat it if he must and was doing
so. But even the best mannered host could not be expected to swill
warm milk. Russell was drinking his normal Nuits St Georges.
When they'd finished they stayed at table, chatting. Jack Pallant
said:

"I envy you greatly. You stuck it for more years than I have and
here you are playing golf and fishing while I'm on boiled chicken
and lukewarm milk."

"The Lord blessed me with an equable temperament."

"And a digestion like a horse."

"You are wrong. A horse has rather a delicate stomach. A couple of horses a little off colour can make the grandest of parades look silly. They're more nuisance than a Light Infantry band."

"Just the same I wish I could stand worry better."

"I've met other men who stand it worse."

"Well . . . One thing went to form at any rate. We've ridden the business of poor James Bullen. At the inquest we couldn't conceal whom he worked for and though most of the papers behaved discreetly the *Gong* began to run it strongly. So we sent for them and had a few words."

"You asked them to lay off?"

"Not at all. The request would only have made them keener. But we pointed out, as a generalisation, that men had been known to visit the Market for reasons other than strictly duty. They couldn't run that – they didn't dare. I know you can't libel a man who is dead but if they printed that without cast iron proof they'd be in trouble inside their own profession. Even the *Gong* has to keep within limits. They killed the story dead next day."

"The inference, as I understand it, being that Bullen was in the Market for women or drugs. Where he ran into a local difficulty as other white men have done before him." Charles Russell frowned and finally said: "A little hard on Bullen's ghost."

"James Bullen was told the rules when he joined."

Charles Russell didn't answer; he couldn't. A commitment to the Security Executive was binding and it was also total. Some men had lost their lives on a mission, several had simply disappeared. Bullen could not complain from his grave that he'd been slandered to conceal an awkward truth.

Jack Pallant took a swig at his milk. "But that aspect apart, the picture is gloomy. There are arms in the country and Ahab wants them. The only way he can get them is through Henshawe. Who wouldn't tell us where they are and won't tell Ahab. Unless, of course, he is *made* to tell. I seriously fear for Henshawe."

"You have a block on him?"

"Of course I have and just as well. Last night there was an

attempt to snatch him. The old taxi routine but the block prevented it."

"Where did it happen?"

"Outside Anne Bullen's block of flats."

"He was calling on her?"

"So it seems. And when the incident had been suitably dealt with he went back to her for the rest of the night."

Charles Russell hid a gentle smile. It had been some years ago but a memorable experience. "But in one way the situation has simplified. It's Ahab versus Henshawe now."

"You call that a simplification?"

"In theory."

"Then what do I do in practice? Tell me."

"You could pull in Henshawe – do the snatching yourself." But it hadn't been said with much conviction.

Nor felt to be a suggestion of merit. Henshawe had been questioned already and had refused a generous accommodation which might well have tempted a different man, and taking his person would have Ahab's own object, which was to force out where the arms were by pain. Charles Russell had never permitted that. The standard dilemma had often been put to him … An aeroplane is flying the skies with three hundred harmless and innocent passengers. On board is a bomb which the crew can't find, on the ground you have the man who put it there … Three hundred lives against one man's agony? Well perhaps, if you could screw yourself up to it. But as a means of routine interrogation torture was totally impermissible. Its use or misuse drew the clearest line between a civilised organisation and a Gestapo.

Jack Pallant seemed to feel the same for he was shaking his head and saying firmly:

"I know you made snatches and I dare say I could, but you made them as a prelude to straightforward disappearances. The people concerned did disappear but they disappeared with a single wound."

"Then what about turning the heat on that girl – the one I now gather is back with Ahab and whom he planted for a time on Henshawe?"

"Barbara Rhys-Harte? She'd probably spill. But it's the arms which matter now first and foremost, not corroborative detail about Ahab's background. And I think we can assume with some safety that the foolish girl knows nothing about them. In the first place Henshawe would hardly have told her, and if he had she in turn would tell Ahab. Who wouldn't in that case be going for Henshawe; he'd be leading us to those weapons directly."

"Sound reasoning," Charles Russell said; he hesitated, then finally said it: "There is one other course."

"I can't wait to hear it."

"You were thinking of strengthening Henshawe's guard?"

Jack Pallant nodded.

"Instead you could simply take them off."

There was a pause while Pallant thought it over. "When Ahab would get hold of Henshawe. When Ahab beats out of him where the arms are. When we simply follow Ahab and collect." He lookd at Russell hard. "Would you?"

"Frankly I would not."

"Then why put it to me?"

"People do have different consciences." Charles Russell was as mild as Pallant's milk.

"Not in this, they don't – they don't indeed. That would make me an accessory to something I wouldn't do directly. If I'm ever obliged to misuse a man I hope I'll have the guts to do it myself."

"Let us leave it, then."

"May I have some more milk?"

Russell sent for it; he was sorry for Pallant. The fashionable word was psychosomatic. A man was put under wicked pressure; he worried and his bowels went wrong; he caught whatever infection was current or in Pallant's case he grew an ulcer. Pallant said:

"Where were we, please?"

"Where we spend more time than we either like – waiting for something to happen to break a deadlock."

"That's very cold comfort."

"I've been there myself."

"I think I shall resign," Pallant said.

"You will do no such foolishness." Charles Russell was for the first time alarmed. He had two good reasons why Pallant should stay. The first was that he had seen this before with other men on a mental rack. Take the pressure off and they ceased to be constipated. In Pallant's case his ulcer would heal.

The second reason was personal and concerned his *protégé*, William Wilberforce Smith. For if Pallant resigned tomorrow morning they would bring in another man from outside, whereas if he completed his term Willy Smith would be older – older and therefore that much more eligible. Willy Smith would have a fair chance of succeeding to what had been Charles Russell's chair.

It was something he devoutly wished to see. He said to Pallant: "You're talking nonsense."

"If you had this thing you wouldn't say so."

"Your ulcer won't get better by sitting at home. I've seen all this before. Believe me."

"Since you're so wise how long have we got to wait?" There'd been more than a hint of friendly irony.

"Till the crisis? I don't know that."

"Yet you lecture me."

"I do no such thing. I'm telling you you're too good to waste."

The words had not been intended as flattery but their effect on Jack Pallant was unexpected. He pushed his milk to one side with distaste and said:

"Do you think I could have a little brandy?"

"You'll pay for it tomorrow morning."

"Or just conceivably not at all."

"Give her a good thump on the bottom and there's no knowing how a woman will take it?"

"I don't think Women's Lib would approve of you."

"I've managed to do pretty well without them."

The lady was of a certain age, expensively dressed and had blue-rinsed hair. She was saying to Ahab distinctly frostily:

"No sir, we cannot help you further. We are a respectable organisation of specialists. That driver should never have had a razor – it was clearly against our rules and he's been dismissed. We are not in the business of common ruffians, far less to make a man talk by beating him. And I have another reason for not wishing to help you. You let us down the first time badly."

137

"*I* let you down?" Ahab sounded astonished. To his mind it was the other way.

"I know what you're thinking but you've no cause for complaint. You should have told us that the man was covered."

"I didn't know."

"Perhaps that is true and perhaps it isn't. In any case you should have suspected. If you didn't you shouldn't be in the business you seem to be." She rose and bowed formally. "Good morning, Mr Ahab. I cannot help further."

She was thinking she wouldn't touch him with firetongs. In her nostrils was the smell of disaster.

Three hours later two men stood before Ahab. They were several rungs down the ladder from the hard men whom he couldn't now find. They were criminals with records, jail-fodder. But they were the best he could hope for in desperation. For a message had come through from his paymaster. Not only was there no question of arms yet but the money too would be reconsidered unless harder and more detailed reports should justify any further payment. Ahab knew what they meant: he'd been dropped. His master had seen some other opening, some more promising chance of creating mischief, but Ahab had not despaired entirely. Simultaneous risings in more than one city were something he could no longer hope for but the Market was still there, the Saviours, and what they might do to London could not be foretold.

With arms, that is. Michael Henshawe's weapons.

Ahab looked at the two men before him with something between disgust and shame. They were out of condition and not too clean; the stench of prison was still about them. But they were all he could now expect or would get.

He was recapping and watching their faces carefully. They seemed to have taken it in, though slowly. "So it has to be tonight or never. Five hundred each if you get what I want."

"Two-fifty in advance," one said.

"I'll make it two hundred."

He passed it over. Blue Rinse had been extremely expensive and it was the last of the money his master had sent him.

Chapter 12

Michael Henshawe too had made his arrangements. The two blacks who ran the furniture van had at first been puzzled but later had laughed. They had helped to move the arms before, more for generous payment than love of subversion, and at first they had protested strongly that any further move was too risky. It had taken some time for the fact to sink in that this time the guns were not their business ... So somebody else was lifting the weaponry, and lifting it with Henshawe's approval? All they were doing was running a decoy, making the fuzz look a pack of fools? When they had got it they both laughed heartily. It was the sort of thing they'd have done for nothing.

So Henshawe had set his alarm clock for midnight, dozing in a chair till it should ring. What woke him was a thud against his front door. He opened it and looked out and froze.

Four men were fighting in bitter silence. Two of them were black, two white. One of the whites was the man in the muffler. Again his absurd pince-nez had fallen and again it seemed to make no difference. The man he was fighting had held a knife but had lost it. Without it he'd also lost his head, rushing Muffler like a bull on rails. Muffler caught his elbows and rolled with the rush. His feet were in the man's stomach, his knees were flexed. The black went over his head in a monkey-climb. He fell very badly, face down and winded. Muffler completed his backwards roll and was on to him in a single movement. The back of his neck was exposed and Muffler hit it with the side of his hand. The black lay still.

With the other two it was over already. The black had had a cosh but now had not. He was lying on the floor in a heap. There'd been a good deal of noise if none of speech but the door of the opposite flat hadn't opened. The area was quietly respectable but uncomfortably close to one which was less so and had adopted its neighbour's first rule of survival. In the case of any kind of trouble you simply hadn't been there to see it.

139

And therefore not to appreciate a classic example of art against muscle.

Muffler looked at the two unconscious blacks, then turned politely to Michael Henshawe. "Good evening, sir. We meet again. May we move that load of rubbish into your flat? Only temporarily of course, while we get our breaths back."

"I cannot stop you," Henshawe said.

"Why should you want to stop us?"

"I'm going out."

"Awkward," Muffler said. "Very awkward." His matter-of-factness was coolly abrasive and Henshawe said sharply:

"Why is it awkward?"

"Because we have to do two things which clash. One is to dispose of these oafies and the other is not to leave you unguarded."

"How are you going to manage the former?"

Muffler said with a gentle patience: "Why, dump them in the Market of course. They're not seriously hurt but they'll stay out for some time. If they recover before they're found they'll melt away, and if they're found it's another Market brawl. That is all perfectly simple – routine. The difficulty is one of logistics since one of us must stay with you. May I ask when you intend to go out?"

Henshawe looked at his watch: it was nearing midnight. To confirm it the alarm clock rang. "Say twenty minutes," he said.

"Not enough."

"Not enough for what?"

"To get a third man to cover you while we dump these two louts. That's not an acceptable risk for a single man. If one of them should come to . . . In a car which the single man will be driving . . . Awkward," Muffler said again. It seemed to be his favourite word.

"Did I hear you speak of a car?"

"You did."

"Then I see no problem at all – I will come with you. If you wish it I will do the driving."

"That would be most obliging."

"Not at all." Henshawe pointed to the two blacks on the landing floor. At no time had they been prepossessing and now one of them had begun to dribble. "I suppose they were going to give me a beating."

"You could put it like that. I would put it stronger."

"Then for the second time I'm in your debt."

The blacks were big men and were running to fat but they got them down the stairs to the car. The smaller they tipped in the boot and locked it, the bigger they propped with Muffler in the back. Henshawe drove with the second guard at his side. Once on the way to the Market the man behind stirred. Muffler hit him again but he struck with mercy.

The Market was entirely deserted for nobody invited a mugging. They drove into a shabby side street which tailed out into a shabbier playground. Muffler said: "Stop, please" and Henshawe stopped. "Turn the car round – this is a cul-de-sac."

Henshawe turned the car obediently, thinking that this man knew his job. He mightn't have thought of that himself and could easily have been caught facing wrongly. "Where do we dump them?"

"Here will do."

They left them on the pavement and drove away. "Seems tough," Muffler said, "but they're not seriously injured. In any case they're not nice men."

Outside Henshawe's flat there was a gap in the parking and a furniture van was backing in neatly. Two blacks got down from the front; they were grinning.

"Good morning, boss. We're bang on time."

"Then I'll join you."

"One moment." It was Muffler, puzzled. "I thought you said you were going out."

"I did and I am. I'm going with these two."

"They're friends of yours?"

"You could call them colleagues."

Muffler didn't like it and said so. "You've had uncomfortably close shaves already. If I were you I'd hide up for a bit – go somewhere safe and keep your head down."

"I've been given that advice before. It's excellent and I mean to take it. When I've done what I have to do tonight."

141

"And what is that?"

"I cannot tell you."

"May I look inside that van?"

"By all means." Henshawe signalled to the blacks. "Open up."

They opened the doors and Muffler looked in. "Empty," he said. "An empty van in the small hours. It smells."

... Excellent. It's meant to smell.

"So now, if I may, I'll join my friends."

"You realise we'll have to follow."

"Please yourselves."

Henshawe said it with a show of indifference but behind it was a real regret. This man had saved him twice from violence and been considerate and courteous in the act. It was a shame to have to make him look foolish. Henshawe got into the van and said: "Off."

The two blacks were feeling no reservations. They were leading the fuzz on the wildest wild goose chase and that would be something to tell their grandchildren. The grinning driver asked:

"Where to?"

"We're not to go west so we'll go to the east. Can you fiddle us through the city on to A.12?"

"I drive round these parts for a living, don't I? When I'm not playing silly games for you."

They moved off and Henshawe looked in the mirror. Behind them were the two guards in the car. "Don't try any tricks. We don't want them to lose us."

They slipped across Blackfriars Bridge to the City. It was busier than Henshawe had expected to find it. Few people were walking these pompous streets but there were cleaning contractors' vans at the kerbs and lorries unloading at the backs of the buildings. Soon they were on to the A.12, moving steadily. Going east there was only a trickle of traffic but in the opposite carriageway were the lorries from Harwich, huge articulated TIRs hauling Dutch red cabbage and Belgian chicory which the English were too lazy to grow.

From time to time Henshawe checked on the following car, twice slowing to let it get back on station. He had the timing worked out precisely. Abdelaziz would need at the most five hours, which meant two and a half each way for Henshawe. Some way past Chelmsford he stopped and turned for home.

It was still dark when they reached the flat again and for the first time the following car drew alongside. Muffler got out and so did Henshawe. The van began to move away. Muffler said to the other guard:

"Go with them."

Henshawe knew that nothing would come of that. The two West Indians were as clean as a soap ad. They had valid licences and a respectable business. They would simply leave the van in its garage and go home for a few hours well-earned sleep. They might have broken the law once before but not tonight. They couldn't be touched and they wouldn't chatter.

Muffler turned sharply to Michael Henshawe. His urbanity had for once deserted him. "I suppose you think you're clever," he said.

"Not clever at all. I just carry out orders."

"And what are you going to do now?"

"Take your advice. I'm going up to pack a bag and after that I'm lying low. Come too if you like and watch me. It's cold."

Michael Henshawe used the telephone first. It was early to wake a sleeping woman and he wasn't entirely sure of Anne's answer. The conventional reply would be 'No' but Anne Bullen was not a conventional woman. Of one thing he was wholly sure: she wouldn't wriggle nor make excuses since she'd never felt the least need to excuse herself.

He told her of the second attempt on him, explaining that it would suit the Executive if he quietly disappeared for a while. She listened in silence, then said:

"Come at once."

He packed two bags and locked the flat. Muffler took one of the bags and they went downstairs. Muffler said a little resentfully:

"A mile before any chance of a taxi."

"I could manage both bags if I had to."

"No. I must see you to wherever you're going."

"Do you want me to tell you?"

"I heard you talking."

"You approve the arrangement?"

"I think it admirable." Muffler's manners had returned with the lightening sky.

"Then I hope I shan't cause you trouble again."

"You won't if you stay inside."

"I mean to."

The two thugs had lain in the street for an hour. A man returning from night shift had seen them, but had done no more than quicken his step, obedient to the local imperative of hearing, saying and seeing nothing. A second passed them by without a glance. The third was a Samaritan, hesitating but finally stopping. He turned them face upwards. They hadn't been cut. He felt their arms and legs. They were whole. Then he, too, went on his way with a shrug.

Chapter 13

Abdelaziz had returned from the pillbox refreshed in body and quiet in mind. He still thought it intelligent to have put back the arms there since very few men would think to look, and the operation had gone like a well-timed staff exercise. When he and the students had arrived in the Market there'd been nobody in the street to watch them; the loading had taken less time than expected; and he was certain that they hadn't been followed. Henshawe had provided a map. No dog had barked, no man had stirred. Moreover he had enjoyed the exercise. He loved the night but could seldom go out in it and had returned to his flat in an excellent temper. So had the students for they had set themselves up. It would be nice to pass their exams if they could but they knew that these were no longer vital. They lived in a patriarchal society and they had obliged a very important man. They would have work for the rest of their lives, that was certain.

And Abdel had almost reached a decision. He had been sent to London with two commissions: the first had been to kill a defector and this he had done without a regret, but the second had been to put pressure on Henshawe and of this he had always had doubts, now multiplied. His respect for Michael Henshawe had grown but not as an effective agent. Moreover his father's scheme had been silly – he was now allowing that word without a pang. A half-sister had been deflowered with a beer bottle, an act of savage, insensate barbarism, but the man had tried to desert and been shot. He hadn't been married, he'd had no brothers, so the blood feud was not in operation. To try to bring down his country in ruins was an over-reaction and therefore foolish.

But Abdel had never been able to say so, or not until now when the picture had changed. He was a feudal man, his father's fiefholder. Impossible to return in failure – worse in open disobedience – but Ahab had utterly changed all that; Ahab was after the weapons and close to them, and Abdel's father would no more arm Ahab then he would the PLO whom he despised. He stood for everything the old man detested, kidnappings, brutal killings, extortion, the mindless urge to destroy good order. So the arms were now safe for another time if his father wouldn't change his mind. Michael Henshawe could be pensioned off, and if his father wouldn't agree to that Abdel himself would find means to do so.

He could return to his country with that; and with honour.

He was homesick again and fiercely wished to. The only man he respected in London was one whom he felt he could not approach, and life in a crowded city frustrated him. In his own country he had to work in the capital with Arabised or Frenchified colleagues whom secretly he looked down on as plainsmen, but every weekend he flew out to the hills. He thought of them now with a bitter nostalgia. He wanted to see his wife again, to talk to his eldest son, to walk his fields. He wanted to breathe sharp air and see open fires, he wanted to watch the barley ripen, to be caught in the sudden storms and see them clear. There were one or two loose ends to tie, but soon, very soon, he'd be going home.

He was happy with these thoughts, half-asleep, when the messenger came in with an envelope. Abdel said a little irritably:

"I take it it's important."

"The *chargé* said so."

Abdelaziz slit the envelope crossly. The message was very short indeed. It said simply that his father was dead.

His first feeling was one of simple relief, for the last of his embarrassments had melted with his father's death. Those weapons, he thought – he needn't retain them; he was no longer in honour bound to retain them against some possible second plan by his father. They could be sent from the country by the road they had entered or perhaps he would drop a hint where it mattered, in which case they'd be quietly collected and if publicised at all (far from certain) attributed to whomsoever was convenient. He would make that decision a little later since at the moment there was one more urgent. He had to get back to his country quickly for there was going to be an immediate power struggle. Abdel didn't want his father's Presidency but he did want to keep a job he enjoyed and he could think of a man who would sweep him away if that man emerged top from the pitiless in-fighting.

146

So his first feeling had been one of relief, but as the messages came in through the morning it changed to one of extreme depression. For his father hadn't died in his bed as Abdel had expected he would. One morning his newest and much younger wife would wake with the old man still warm beside her. She was a sensible girl and must long have expected it, so she wouldn't make the tearful fuss which an Arab woman would feel was obligatory. Instead she would dress and send for the doctor. She was carrying the old man's son; she'd be cared for.

But Abdel's father hadn't died like that, he had died in the sort of senseless killing which he had always stonily set his face against. He hadn't been a religious man but he had valued all roots and established customs and on Friday he had gone to prayers. He had gone alone, without precedence and unguarded, and had been praying in the third or fourth row. And in the fifth or sixth a man had risen and shot him in the back of the neck. There hadn't been instant pandemonium for the mosque where the men had been praying was holy, and one didn't compound one great sin with another. The man had been quietly hustled outside and there he had been cut to pieces. A single policeman had looked the other way.

That was bad enough but worse had followed for while the man had still had a head to shout from he had shouted the slogans of his political credo, and what was left of him had soon been identified. He had a record of political trouble-making and like Ahab had been in a local prison. He was undoubtedly an Ahab in politics and he was also one of Ahab's race.

He owned no kin in Abdel's country.

Abdel had realised what that meant instantly and had swung from relief into shocked despair. The ball and chain of the old man's plan had been struck from him by his father's death only for another to grip him. What held him now was inescapable, the fetter of the ancestral blood feud. It wasn't a matter of mental conviction nor even a plain desire for revenge; it was as much a part of his being as his bowels.

He began to consider how to kill Ahab. He could find out where he lived and go there; he could shoot him and with reasonable luck he could be out of the country before he was caught. But he turned this down at once as bad manners. The English hadn't treated him shabbily and though he mightn't be caught he would surely be traced. When the English would think, and perfectly rightly, that he'd grossly abused their hospitality. He was also an accredited diplomat with obligations as well as outrageous privileges. He couldn't bring himself to behave like an Arab.

No, he'd have to set a trap for Ahab and the bait for that trap was those arms in the pillbox. But he couldn't do that alone, he needed help. If anything went wrong as it might Ahab would walk away with the weapons ... The police? No, the police might have turned a blind eye when it suited them and they would surely be pleased to lay hands on the hardware, but they wouldn't lend aid to an open killing.

But the Executive might – Ahab's death would oblige them. They weren't above the law but they bent it. Abdel would have to call on Charles Russell after all.

He considered which would better come first, set the snare for Ahab or talk to Russell. Finally he tossed a coin and the coin came down to send for Ahab.

The letter had come by an embassy messenger and all Ahab's instincts were screaming 'Trap'. He knew how Abdel's father had died and he knew the man who had coldly killed him. He thought him a fool but that wasn't the point: the point was that the man was a terrorist and Ahab was a terrorist too. To go to that embassy, foreign soil, would be an action of sheerest desperation.

On the other hand Ahab *was* desperate. He had long since guessed where Henshawe's arms came from, and though the letter hadn't mentioned weapons it had talked of a matter of mutual interest. Well, he wasn't going to get arms out of Henshawe. Henshawe had been effectively guarded and had now been smuggled away into hiding. But Ahab had to have weapons or fail.

For time was running against him faster than ever. FAAR was falling to pieces around him and FAAR was his essential cover. He had a work permit but only for FAAR and as an alien they could deport him easily. And FAAR was not the only thing crumbling: his cells were showing signs of that too. Their members were resentful and bitter and in violence they would still be incalculable, but they weren't disciplined men who would hold together. He had to give them arms or see them collapse.

To be so near, he thought. So near, so near ...

Like Abdel he tossed a coin and it came down 'Go.'

But one thing he did before he went. If this were a trap he'd take some of them with him. He took his pistol from a drawer and called a cab.

Abdel received him with solemn courtesy. He offered a drink which Ahab declined and opened the conversation by saying:

"I don't think you often carry a firearm."

"Why do you say that?"

"I can see it. So did the doorman who rang me at once. I told him to let you keep it. But you should carry it in a shoulder-holster, it's far too big for a pocket of any kind. In any case, you will find no need for it."

"I'm glad to hear that."

"Then let us come to the point. You don't mind if I'm blunt?"

"I prefer it," Ahab said.

"So be it. Then you are interested in an assortment of weapons which were once held by a Mr Henshawe, from whom you tried to extort them without success."

"How do you know that?"

"Because he told me. Henshawe was my agent. A poor one. I expect you have guessed all that."

"More or less."

"Henshawe no longer holds those arms. They are back in my possession safely."

Ahab rose at once. "Then I'll go. But it was kind of you to warn me."

"Please sit down. I didn't call you here to warn you but to discuss a possible mutual advantage."

"In the circumstances I do not see one."

"Possibly not. But I do. Clearly. The future use of those arms in this country."

Time ebbed away for perhaps two minutes, then Ahab said slowly:

"I do have connections."

"That too I have known for some time. Are they good ones?"

"They are capable of using arms but they're a volatile, unreliable people."

"Which means that the clock's ticking loudly against you."

"I had realised it," Ahab said.

Abdel had considered his next move carefully. Whatever else Ahab was he was a pro; he would respect another, even an enemy; he might not respect or trust a diplomat.

"Do you know what I do here?"

"I know you're a counsellor."

"I am also still head of the Private Bureau. It wasn't I who jailed you once but the man who then held the chair I now sit in."

"I'm sorry about those two jailors. I had to."

... An extraordinary man but not quite an animal.

"I was sent here with two separate duties. The first was to kill a traitor which I have done. The second was to expedite Henshawe in the task which my father had mistakenly given him. That aspect I have now abandoned. Henshawe is entirely unqualified for a duty which he assumed too lightly. Against that my father's orders still bind me."

It was the first lie of the morning but also credible. Ahab would be too clever for foolish ones.

He saw that he must make the next move. It was a big one but he must make it sometime. "The proposition?" he enquired and waited.

"Those arms. In your hands. To do as you wish with."

The next question was not polite but natural. "And what do you get out of that?"

"The satisfaction of a duty completed." It came out as smoothly as though the truth. Abdel could see that Ahab was nibbling.

He had in fact done more than nibble; he was near to taking the bait in a gulp.

"You mean you will give me those arms?"

"I do." Abdel produced a map and a key. "You will find them in a decaying pillbox."

"And when do I collect them?"

"When you please." Abdel had foreseen the question and also how to answer it wisely. Show the least sign of interest once the key had passed hands and Ahab would know there was something suspicious. Abdel rubbed this in by saying casually:

"I have no interest in how you operate. None."

Ahab rose to his feet. "May I thank you?"

"No. I cannot pretend I like your kind but my first duty is to my father's ghost."

This time it wasn't a lie but the truth. His father's ghost wouldn't rest in its grave if the body from which it had come went unavenged.

Chapter 14

Abdelaziz had taken a great deal of pains with the letter that he had written to Russell, deciding, before he had even drafted it, that it must somehow combine three disparate threads which weren't by their natures the easiest weaving. To begin with it must be properly respectful – not subservient, Russell would be annoyed by subservience – but conveying that the writer realised that though he was head of a Private Bureau that made him at the most a colleague; he couldn't and didn't presume to equality. And then there was the difficulty that he was already in Charles Russell's debt; he wasn't coming to repay a kindness but openly to seek another, and this after something like forty years with no stronger personal contact than Christmas cards. Finally the matter was urgent and if you tried to push a man like Russell he was as likely as not to show you the door.

The third draft, Abdel thought, would do, and he faired it in his careful italic and sent it to Russell's flat by a messenger. An hour later Abdel's telephone rang. Colonel Russell would be delighted to see him . . . When? At any time convenient. Why not now?

He let out a sigh of relief; he'd been lucky. The answer had been quick and decisive but a 'No' would have been equally prompt. Russell was not a man to dither but nor was he one to act impetuously.

And indeed he had given the matter thought. He liked to keep the past in its place, a not unsatisfying background to the evening of his life. Digging up old bones was inelegant. And apart from any doubts in principle there were the brutally concrete facts of what Abdel had done. Very probably he had shot down Maoui, though this wasn't a matter which much disturbed Russell, but he had sent in arms in the Bag and that did. Those arms were now in a place unknown and there wasn't any lead to their whereabouts. In certain hands they could spell disaster. Russell knew of this because Pallant had told him. Did Abdel know that? It seemed improbable.

Then why was he coming? The make-or-break question. It was possible Abdel had changed his mind, that he didn't intend to use those weapons but planned to turn them in and go home. After all his job was good order and discipline: security men seldom worked with subversives. But there was more than one way of doing that without calling on the ex-head of the Executive. And the letter had spoken, with proper apology, of asking a favour, not offering to do one.

Charles Russell had considered carefully. For instance, should he call Pallant in? No. If something went wrong he himself would be vulnerable but Abdel, if he had wanted to, could easily have made contact with Pallant, and the presence of another man, particularly such a man as Pallant, could inhibit Abdel as nothing else would. This was going to be on a personal basis or it was going to be nothing at all, a flop. There were arms floating round the country, a menace . . .

He rang Abdel and told him he'd see him whenever he liked . . . At once? Yes, at once.

Russell drank two whiskies rather faster than usual. He was presuming that Abdel didn't drink and if his housekeeper had a single fault it was that she made indifferent coffee.

Abdel came in and they shook hands formally. "This is a very great honour indeed."

"I'm flattered you have come to see me."

Russell had expected formality, since Abdel didn't come of a race which considered familiarity seemly, and he was prepared to thaw the ice out slowly. "It's been too long since we met," he said.

"And now that we meet again I feel ashamed."

"I can't think why."

"You did me a great service once and I should be coming here to repay your kindness. Instead I am asking another favour. It is true that I can repay this second but the original will still stand to my debit."

"I don't think of it like that."

"I must."

'Must', Russell thought, had been used precisely. They came from different civilisations but there were values which both respected equally. The words for them were abomination to every

154

kind of progressive thinking for they were a roll-call of the old-fashioned virtues: discipline, order and personal honour.

Such as paying a debt if one possibly could.

"May I tell you why I am here in England?"

"Please do."

Abdel began to tell his story and Russell listened in total silence. He started at the beginning and told it well. Russell could have saved him trouble by telling him there was much that he knew, but there could be only one source of his previous knowledge and he didn't wish to compromise Pallant by admitting they'd been in touch already. Pallant might be needed later when the really high cards had gone down on the table.

So he listened but used the time to reflect, to remember how he had first met Abdel.

They had been fighting their way up the spine of Italy against desperate and often savage resistance, a polyglot army but brilliantly led. Major Russell had been lightly wounded and had been sent down the line for the doctors to deal with him. He was returning now with his soldier servant and the soldier servant was driving the Jeep. The L of C troops were French colonials and Russell knew their curious history. Many were, strictly speaking, deserters, having slipped away from their proper units when they'd learnt that these had thrown in with Vichy, joining others which had gone a different way. Major Russell had the greatest respect for them. Some of their customs were not his own but they were fine fighting men if poorly officered.

The village through which they were driving now had been shelled into the ground in a battle, but as the tide of war rolled further north the villagers had returned to their ruins. And in the square there was some sort of disturbance. It was blocking the road and Russell stopped. A priest detached himself from the crowd.

"Can you speak Italian?"

"A little." In fact Charles Russell spoke it well.

"There's going to be a murder. Please stop it."

"What sort of a murder?"

"Judicial murder." The priest began to gabble hysterically, slipping into the local dialect. "These colonial troops are pretty rough and we've had to complain of several rapes. The French have decided they'll have to crack down on it. Summary court martial and shot on the spot." He pointed to what was left of his church. Outside it stood two sheepish women, a French colonial soldier and a lieutenant in an ill-kept *képi*. The lieutenant appeared to have lost his head. He was shouting and waving a large revolver. The priest said: "Those women complain they've been raped by that soldier."

"But I can't interfere in that."

"You should. The women are the village whores."

Charles Russell thought it over, said: "I'm an officer in the British army. That lieutenant is a Frenchman."

"But I tell you those women are whores."

"Too bad."

The priest spat on the ground and turned his back.

Russell said to his driver: "Come with me. Come with me and bring your weapon."

They pushed their way through the crowd to the church. Russell looked first at the colonial soldier. He was young and understandably frightened but he was bearing himself with a simple dignity. Russell said to the Frenchman:

"What goes on?"

Who swung on him still waving the pistol. "And who in hell are you?"

"Good question. You could call me just a passer-by."

"Then mind your own business."

"I wish I could."

The Frenchman looked at Russell's crown. "I recognise your rank," he said, "but not your right to give me orders."

Russell looked back at the Frenchman, puzzled. He liked to be able to place his adversaries and this one fitted no slot he knew. St Cyr was ruled out by the shabby uniform, which to Russell was no disadvantage, and the man was hardly old enough to be some species of promoted ranker which would have won his instant respect and attention. His father must be high in the *patronat*, the son a placeman in a defeated army which the despised Anglo-Saxons had twice had to rescue.

"Perfectly correct. I agree."

Russell had been intending to cool it but his calmness shredded the last of the Frenchman's control.

"Get out of here before I shoot you."

Russell raised a hand to his driver. It was warm but he was wearing gloves. The driver carried a slung machine pistol and the click as he slid the safety-catch was audible.

The Frenchman went white and for the first time stopped shouting. Russell used the moment to talk on collectedly:

"I think you should make a few more enquiries. This priest here" – he waved at him – "says those women are prostitutes."

"You believe him?"

"We can soon corroborate." He looked at the soldier who was still standing silently. "What language does that soldier speak?"

"They all of them know a little Arabic."

"Then ask him how much he paid the women."

The Frenchman said in a small voice: "I cannot."

"You mean that you know no Arabic?"

"None. I am not an officer of the colonial army."

Charles Russell thought but did not say, that this man should not be commissioned at all. "Does he understand French?"

"Drill French. No more."

Charles Russell pulled his moustache reflectively. This was an impasse and Russell knew it. But his driver unexpectedly said:

"I've picked up a few words of wog, sir."

"Then try them on that man. How much?"

The driver spoke terrible barrack-room Arabic but the soldier seemed to understand him. The soldier said to Russell: "Five dollars, sir. For some reason he's being paid in American so he gave them five oncers."

"Then if they've got five oncers on them they're whores."

"I don't think we ought to search them, sir."

"I don't propose to have them searched." Russell turned to the women and switched to Italian. "This man says he bought you."

They shrilly protested. They were respectable women, one of them married, and they'd been savagely and brutally raped. The priest at Russell's side said again: "They're whores."

Russell finally made his mind up and acted; he said to the women:

"*Fuori la grana.*"

157

The tone of voice had been sharply authoritative but it was the colloquialism which turned the scale. One of the women put her hand in her bosom. It came out with five single dollar bills. She threw them on the ground in disgust. Charles Russell picked them up and gave them back. He turned to the Frenchman, not concealing contempt:

"If you'll take my advice you'll learn your men's language."

And now this simple but stoical soldier was a powerful man who was telling his tale – Maoui's treachery to his father's plan, how Ahab had an organisation but not the arms to make it effective, how Ahab was desperate for Henshawe's weapons, how Abdel had therefore taken them back from him. Charles Russell did not interrupt him till he finally spoke of his father's death.

"I was very sorry to hear of that. I never had the honour of meeting him but I admired him from a distance, very much."

"He was too formidable to speak of love but I was proud to be his son and still am. That is why I have come to you since, inescapably, I am bound to avenge him."

Charles Russell returned to a studied silence. On the blood feud he was somewhat equivocal. It was savage but, like duelling, defensible. In a certain sort of civilisation it was cleaner than going to courts which were corrupt. It was also less expensive to the state. After some time he said defensively:

"That strikes me as your private business."

"It certainly is and I cannot delegate. And to do it with honour I must do it alone. I haven't come here to ask for assistance."

"Then for what?" It was sharp.

"Let us call it a guarantee of neutrality. And for that I am prepared to pay."

"In what coin?"

"Those arms. Since my father is dead I'm not bound by his wishes, only to avenge his death. I told you I had recovered the weapons. I know where they are but so does Ahab."

"How does Ahab know?"

"I told him. I also gave a good reason for doing so. I said in effect that since Henshawe had failed us my father would wish him to act instead. In fact he would have died before doing so but Ahab had no means of knowing that. I threw a bait and Ahab took it."

"So it's Ahab you mean to kill?"

"Who else?" Abdel explained with the first hint of impatience. "The man who murdered my father had no sons. Nor did he have relations close enough to be seemly to pick on them to atone." (The rules, Russell thought, are plainly established. They don't appear to me to be unfair.) "But Ahab is a terrorist and so was the man who gunned down my father. Moreover he was one of Ahab's race."

Charles Russell was impressed but concealed it. He thought of duelling again and its encrusted code. What he was hearing could be described as barbarous but it couldn't properly be called illogical. Perhaps he should slam this door at once but there were arms at stake, men's lives, huge disorder . . . He said at last:

"Go on."

"With pleasure. I set my snare for Ahab last night. All I want to know from Pallant is when he moves. I shall move faster and be there first. Pallant in turn will follow Ahab and he'll be leading him to where those arms are."

"But what is to stop him doing that anyway? Almost certainly Ahab is tailed already."

For the first time Abdelaziz looked surprised. "I don't think you understand what drives me. If Pallant cannot agree to my plan Ahab is still going to die but less secretly. He might die publicly and messily and I am an accredited diplomat."

"You could call that blackmail."

"I prefer *quid pro quo*."

"But how secret is it going to be? Bodies are not disposed of so easily."

"They can be if you have time to plan it." He began to relax again, one professional to another. "A man in my embassy has been sick for several weeks. He has been regularly attended by an Indian doctor −"

"I'm beginning to get it."

"Perhaps not quite all of it. The man died last night or rather he didn't. He flew out of the country on a passport we bought for him. Nobody showed any interest. Why should they? What we are left with is a valid death certificate."

"I bet that cost a packet."

"It did. We are also left with a suitable coffin. The officially deceased was extremely pious and wished to lie in his native soil. We shall send Ahab out with honours he hasn't earned."

"I've heard of that one before. It can come unstuck. That Indian doctor –"

"Got more than money. He was told that if he spoke he was dead. Bengalis believe in an after-life but they're rather less eager to die than many."

"You've thought it all out."

"No, I've gone by the book."

Russell walked to the sitting room window and looked at the street. Outside it had begun to snow. Two Indians scurried by, heads down. Charles Russell half-believed in omens and if this were one it was probably good. He returned to his chair.

"So what do I do?"

"I realise you cannot authorise this."

"You realise rightly."

"But you can put it to Pallant with more hope than I could."

"Then let's have the basics again to be sure of them."

"Ahab will lead you to where the arms are. I have no further use for them. You have. The sole condition is very simple, that you do not interfere between me and Ahab."

Charles Russell said: "I will put that to Pallant."

Abdelaziz rose at once. "I am still ashamed. It is I should be doing you a service."

"Those weapons would be a very great service."

"But they do not expunge a personal debt."

"You're a man of very strict principles, aren't you?"

"Yes," Abdel said, "I suppose I am." He held out his hand. They were back to formality. "I doubt if we shall meet again."

"It does seem unlikely. I greatly regret it."

When Abdel had gone Charles Russell laughed softly. They were certainly going to meet again unless Pallant turned the whole thing down and Russell was fairly sure he would not. They were going to meet again and soon.

It was going to be the sort of evening which an old war horse wouldn't miss for a million.

Chapter 15

An hour later Charles Russell was talking to Pallant. Jack Pallant
was pulling a face and saying:

"I don't much like it."

"I didn't really suppose you would."

"I know where you yourself stood on killings. If they were
necessary they were undertaken but you insisted that you alone
gave the order. This one is simply standing aside, making me a
dim accessory."

"I told you that Ahab was going to die anyway. Abdel doesn't
share our ethos but he's a diplomat from a state we keep in with. If
he shoots down Ahab publicly we're up the creek."

"He also sounds uncomfortably clever."

"Just call him a hard old stone like myself."

Jack Pallant said: "I need a drink."

"I'd like one very much myself."

They both took long pulls before Russell went on. "I'm going to
ask an unfair question. Would you like to see Ahab dead?"

"Of course."

"Then would you be prepared to order it?"

"Not on what we know at the moment. If he got those arms I
might very well have to."

"If he got those arms you'd be acting too late."

Pallant looked at Charles Russell with a certain resentment. "I
wish you weren't so bloody logical."

"In this case the logic is also persuasive. You're getting two
birds with one stone without throwing. Ahab's an international
terrorist and if he doesn't succeed in England he'll try elsewhere.
And those arms in the wrong hands could mean revolution, or if
that sounds a little melodramatic just call it armed rioting in
several towns."

"It's a pretty stark dilemma."

"On the contrary I think you're lucky."

"You have a rum idea of luck."

"My own."

Pallant began to pace the room and Russell lit his evening cigar. "If we only knew *now* where Ahab was going –"

"We could get there first and swipe the lot? But Abdel is much too acute to have told me that."

"And what about the body we find?"

"My friend, we do not find a body. Abdelaziz, as I said, is a pro."

Pallant said sincerely: "He sounds one." He returned to his chair and drummed on the table. "So as I see it the party goes something like this. I tell you when Ahab moves out of London and you in turn pass the news to Abdel. Abdel knows where the arms are – he won't need to tail Ahab – but he'll be waiting at the baited trap. We are permitted to follow Ahab, something we should have done in any case, but with the certain knowledge of what he is up to and time to make our arrangements accordingly. The price of that admitted service is to turn a blind eye on a blood feud killing." He stood up suddenly. "Charles, would *you*?"

"I don't like to talk about duty lightly."

Pallant said: "Damn you, damn you, damn you."

Charles Russell went home in a taxi contentedly. Pallant had been a senior policeman and he hadn't expected to sway him easily but now that he had he was totally confident. Pallant would handle the details competently, there wouldn't be any silly slip-ups. He'd send a single good man, very probably Willy, with instructions not to interfere till Abdel had done what Abdel must. What else he would do would depend on Ahab who would almost certainly come alone. The first time, that is, and there would not be another. Abdel had baited his hook with cunning but Ahab was a man of experience; however credible the reason given, however enormous the glittering prize, he could never be quite sure that there wasn't a snare. Time running against him, sheer desperation, would drive him to take that chance himself but he wouldn't take other men with him until he knew.

Charles Russell was thinking of bed when the phone rang. "I have a message for your friend Abdelaziz. Ahab is moving tonight and alone."

162

"You're sure of that?"

"As sure as I can be. I read it as a preliminary reconnaissance. We've been shadowing him for quite a while and we know that he hasn't hired heavy transport. But he has hired a car until midday tomorrow and it's standing outside his flat at the moment."

"When do you think he'll go?"

"When would you?"

"There isn't a moon and they've promised us snow again. I'd time it to be there at first light. When I'd check and depart without touching a thing. Later, when the weather lifts —"

"I think you're right."

"Then I'll pass this to Abdel."

When he had done so Charles Russell did not undress. Instead he went to his lock-up and fetched his car; he filled the tank at an all-night garage and then left the car outside his flat. Inside he checked again with his diary. First light would be just before six o'clock and in the early snow which had been ominously forecast he'd allow two hours for the journey. That would give him three hours in a chair and he set his alarm. But before sleeping he made his careful arrangements. He found his heaviest overcoat, an ancient *posteen* which he'd brought from India; he made sandwiches and a Thermos of coffee and he put with them a half-bottle of brandy. He wasn't of a seemly age to go walking about in the snow at dawn but since he had decided to do so he would make sure that he didn't freeze to death.

He was confident that he knew where the arms were. He'd been impressed by Abdel's cool professionalism and professionals mostly chose the book answer, something used before and success-fully like the routine of a coffin and switching bodies. That had been a clue to Abdel's mind. The hardware had had to be taken from Henshawe and Abdel wouldn't risk bringing it back to his embassy. To find another Henshawe to hide it would be difficult to do in practice and moreover offend the basic rule of the fewer people who knew the better. Russell didn't think, as had Abdel, that his choice would be a criminal cliché; he had thought of what he would do himself and he hadn't had a doubt about that. Estab-lished professionals preferred the established.

163

He had already done his map-reading carefully and had decided against an approach by the towpath. That had been good enough for Willy Smith who was young and had also had a moon but for Russell it would be simple folly. Instead he'd come in through the belt of new building, the development beyond the railway line.

He parked his car and began to walk. There were two others but they told him nothing. There wasn't a light in the dull little houses and the snow showers had increased in frequency. At the end of the street was a level-crossing giving access to the fields beyond the line. It was an unmanned crossing and at night was kept open. Beyond it was a gate which Russell swung. He shut it behind him and put his torch on his compass. If he walked north-east he would hit the pillbox.

A man rose from nowhere and put a gun in his stomach. Charles Russell said:

"Good morning, Willy."

William Wilberforce Smith stood silently, staring. He didn't appear to believe what he saw. At last he managed speech:

"How did you know?"

"I didn't know in the sense I could prove it or I might have felt obliged to tell Pallant. But I've been in this game for much longer than he has and that time has given me certain insights into minds which work a certain way. It isn't important but here I am. Since *you're* here I take it Ahab's here too."

"Ahab hasn't arrived yet."

"Then how – ?"

"Pallant decided to put me on Abdel who was going to the same place anyway. If Ahab had happened to spot me he might have funked it. Abdel wouldn't care a damn and in fact we exchanged 'good mornings' parking our cars."

... Admirable thinking. Cool.

"Where is he now?"

"I'm afraid I've lost him. He's wearing white ski clothes and moving around. He had a rifle when he left his car."

"We suspect he used one once before."

"Have you a weapon, sir?"

"Certainly not. I don't carry arms when I go to a play. And talking of plays let's settle for where we are."

They lay down in the snow and Russell said: "I gather you've been here before."

"Not in snow."

"Then you'd better have a drink before you freeze." He produced coffee and the half-bottle of brandy.

"You think of everything, sir."

"I'm older than you are."

They lay in the powdery snow uncomfortably. Once Russell thought he had seen Abdelaziz but he was moving like a ghost in his native hills. Presently Willy held up a hand. There was the sound of a car in the street beyond the line. They could see its lights but these went out. Willy said:

"Ahab."

"A very good bet."

In the east the sky had begun to lighten and as Ahab came through the gate they could make him out. He left the gate open behind him and walked on.

"Not a countryman," Russell said disapprovingly.

"But he's getting a better target with every step."

Russell wondered how Abdel was going to handle it. He had thought once that the rules seemed fair but how fair they were he didn't know. Abdel's father had been shot in the back: it might be perfectly proper to do the same. But Russell rather doubted it would be. The light was getting steadily stronger.

Ahab walked to the pillbox and opened it. He went inside; came out; and relocked it. He began to walk back towards the gate.

Abdel rose in his path and called his name. He had a rifle at the ready and not yet aimed. Ahab fumbled but pulled his pistol. There was an instant from a spaghetti Western, then two shots and both men fell. After a moment one got up slowly.

Charles Russell and Willy walked across to him. If Russell had expected surprise Abdelaziz showed none whatever. He pointed down at Ahab contemptuously.

"He's a rotten shot."

"But I see he winged you." Abdel's whole weight was on one leg.

"He hit me in the foot."

"So I see. It's lucky you have a venal doctor."

"The doctor comes later — just now there's a problem. He's a pretty big man but I reckoned to carry him. Slung across my shoulder, I thought. But now with a gammy leg I cannot."

Russell said at once: "We could help you."

"That's really very kind indeed." He might have been accepting a light.

Russell and Willy lifted Ahab and Abdel limped alongside across the line. There were now four cars and Abdel chose one of them, opening the boot.

"Tip him in."

They tipped him.

Abdel shut the boot and came round to the driver's door. Russell asked:

"Can you drive?"

"I can use my heel."

"You're not losing blood?"

"A little. But I'll last."

He climbed into the car and said: "I'm more embarrassed than ever now. I doubt if I'll live long enough to have very much chance of repaying your kindnesses."

Russell said only: "Go with God."

When Abdel had gone Russell turned to Willy. There were now three cars in the deserted street. He pointed at one. "That's mine. Which is yours?"

"The green one."

"So the red was Ahab's. What are you going to do about that?"

"It's hired until twelve o'clock this morning. We'll be collecting and discreetly returning it as soon as it is properly light."

"Ten out of ten," Russell said. "Let's go home."

Chapter 16

Mrs Alderney Cohn had a largish mail for she wrote many letters of no great importance to persons who were of similar mind, and most of these replied at length that yes, they must somehow build a bridge between the social failure of orthodox communism and the corrupt and capitalist transatlantics. But a letter had come through the box this morning which she hadn't expected and didn't like. It was an invitation from a Mr Jack Pallant to visit him at her earliest convenience.

Her first thought was to refuse out of hand since the Executive stood for all she detested, the continuing fight to support the established, whatever was old and tried and of good repute. But on reflection she realised this might be unwise. She didn't believe the stories she circulated about the Executive being a secret Gestapo, but she guessed it could be a formidable enemy whom it would be sensible to placate if she could. She telephoned and made an appointment.

Pallant received her with gentle courtesy. He offered her tea which she brusquely refused. "I'm a busy woman," she said. She was pompous.

"So I have always understood. I'll make it as short as I can." He caught and held her eyes unwaveringly. "Did you know what Ahab really did?"

It had been on the tip of her tongue to ask where he was but now she swallowed the question as futile. It had been intended as an embarrassment since she hadn't expected a truthful answer but the man before her was quietly confident. Such a question wouldn't unsettle him in his chair. He would merely think her naive and she'd go one down. She decided to answer what this quiet man was asking her.

"He came to us with a recommendation from a member whom I need not name. He seemed eminently suitable so FAAR took him on."

"Did you know he had a criminal record? Not in this country yet, but outside it."

"No, I did not." It was true but she saw her position had weakened. She decided to tell a little more of the truth. "Towards the end of his service I had started to wonder. He did his job but was often absent."

"Were you not suspicious?"

"Of what? I must remind you I am not a policeman." For a moment she thought she had got a hole back but Pallant merely said:

"Nor am I. Sometimes I wish I was back where I came from."

He gave her his crocodile grin for he'd made up his mind. The word 'understanding' had not been uttered, but on it a pact had been reached which would hold. She wouldn't pursue what had happened to Ahab and he wouldn't pursue what she knew of his doings. She confirmed his decision by saying casually:

"Talking of Ahab, he's disappeared. I imagine he has left the country."

"I imagine very much the same thing."

She started to reach for her bag but he stopped her. "You said you were a busy woman. But not so busy as once you were."

She saw that it was useless to fence with him; he had a stronger wrist and more behind it. "You are referring to FAAR? It is going downhill."

"I understand it is as good as bankrupt."

"You have excellent information."

"I need it. I also know you're a wealthy woman."

"If you suspect I'd shore up FAAR you must be mad."

"My private guess was that you would not. But I'm grateful for the confirmation."

When she had gone he took a list from the safe. It was a list of similar organisations which his masters considered public nuisances. He crossed out FAAR which left three to go. All of them were apparently innocent and all of them covered for something less so.

Next time, he thought, I may not be lucky.

Barbara Rhys-Harte had worked it out. The Foundation had told her they could no longer afford her and she hadn't offered to work for nothing. Ahab had gone and her interest with him. She

168

assumed he had made some slip and they'd run him out. He wouldn't write and she didn't wish it. Doctor Ahab had done his business: she was free.

And her mother's health was getting worse which would give her an excuse if she wanted one. In fact she did not for she had decided already. She was going back home as a county grandee. The north of Pembrokeshire was self-consciously Welsh but the south had been fairly evenly anglicised. Little England beyond Wales, they called it, and if you had land and the money to work it, it was a life which any sane woman would envy.

With a suitable partner, of course, but she'd thought of that too. She was going to marry the local vicar who had shown signs that he wasn't a natural celibate ... Squiress and the parish priest. It was something out of a Trollope novel but not a whit the worse for that. At first there might be certain difficulties since his reverence was a nephew of Crondal's and she'd heard rumours that he shared his tastes. But she'd soon put a stop to any nonsense of that sort. Therapy was the word in fashion and she had the experience to dispense it competently.

And she'd have to be fairly quick about it. His first-born wouldn't resemble him closely but there wouldn't be a thing he could do. Bent Anglican clergy were natural cuckolds.

His deputy had come to the airport to meet him and Abdel limped out into wintry sunshine. He did nothing dramatic like kissing the tarmac but was delighted to be home and showed it. The struggle for power on his father's death had been won by a man he knew and respected, a grandson of one of his grandmother's cousins. His own position was therefore safe. His deputy said:

"Glad to have you back." He was not an intriguer and Abdel believed him. He handed Abdelaziz a letter. "From the President," he said; he allowed a smile "But you needn't bother to open it now. It's congratulations and fourteen days' leave. The Presidential helicopter is waiting on its pad at your service. I think I can guess where you mean to go."

As they walked towards the chopper the deputy said: "In your absence I've had to do the adding. I've been looking at a disappearance in England and at a coffin which arrived by air. Also at your regrettable accident. My conclusion was the figure of three."

"Let us forget it."

"It is already forgotten. But I'd have done the same myself and been proud to."

The helicopter flew up to the hills and Abdel went first to his father's grave. He had been buried as he had wished to be, simply, lying in peace in his native earth. Abdel began to pray beside the grave. He had earned the right to do so. His conscience was clear.

At his house his son knelt down for his blessing. He was a man nearing forty and had made Abdel a grandfather.

"Nowadays that's a little old-fashioned."

"It happens to be the way I like it."

Michael Henshawe was telling Anne Bullen quietly:

"Abdel has been here while you were out. He tells me it's perfectly safe to move. I don't know how to thank you."

"Don't try." She added with an ironic primness: "I've very much enjoyed your visit."

He had excellent reason to know this was true and went on with an increasing confidence. "I'm the sort who needs steady company badly."

"That goes for me too. And many of them."

"Does it have to be many?"

She looked at him coolly, not unprepared. "That would really depend on what I got for my money."

"I was thinking of getting married."

"What on?" The question came with a Dutch brutality but the Bullens had served Dutch William intimately and Netherlands' genes were notoriously long-lived.

"I've got a job here – not a bad one."

"I never thought you'd serve the Bull."

"I'm not serving the English, I'm serving Abdel."

"Spying on us lot?" She didn't like it.

"Not spying – I'm not even a diplomat. Abdel's country wants to boost trade with this one so they've bought the house next door to their consulate. There'll be promotions and exhibitions – the works."

"But you don't know the first thing about trade."

"That's exactly what I said to Abdel. He doesn't often smile but for once he laughed."

"What did he say when he wasn't laughing?"

"That it wouldn't be the first time I had taken on something I hadn't been trained for."

"And a fine dog's dinner you made of the last one."

"I said that too but he said I'd learn quickly. One of his kinsmen is going to keep shop and I'm to do the legwork and contacts. It's pretty generously paid."

"He sounds a generous man."

"He is. He said I'd been loyal when I might have been otherwise and for that I deserved what he was pleased to call dirty money. It was a considerable capital sum, worth investing. But I'm keeping a little aside for emergencies."

"Have you any in mind?"

"Only one."

"What's that?"

He told her and she thought for a minute. "All right," she said finally. "Let's go and buy it."

Amanda and Willy had finished supper and were sitting on the sofa holding hands. Willy wasn't an enormous eater except when she served up something with rice and tonight there had been jumbalaya. He had eaten a good deal more than usual and was sitting with her replete and somnolent.

"Did you get that rice in the Market?"

"Why do you ask? I thought they'd taken you off the Market for good."

"There's nothing more to do there so they have. But I still have a sort of second-hand interest."

"If you want to know whether it's peaceful it is. If some bobby does something silly again I dare say there'll be another riot but the underlying strain has gone."

"No more talk of the Saviours?"

"If you mention them people shrug and laugh. They were sinister once like some of the Rastas but now they're one of yesterday's jokes." She was suddenly alert and suspicious. "You're not thinking of poking about again?"

"I told you – there's nothing left to poke for. But I got myself a good mark for what there was."

"I'm glad," she said, and squeezed his hand. She knew he had ambitions and shared them.

"I've got an extra week's leave so where shall we go?"

"What about the baby?"

"Mother was a nurse – she'd love him."

She was tempted, half-hooked. "But not abroad."

"I wasn't thinking of going abroad. Why not Brighton again? I remember it was where you seduced me."

"If I hadn't," she said, "I'd have blown wide open." She added on a faint note of complacency: "It was quite a weekend."

"It was indeed. I don't think we ever went down to the restaurant."

She laughed at that and said: "So it's Brighton."

"But there's something about the Brighton air."

She knew what he meant and unexpectedly giggled. They had gone to Brighton two and come back three. "That might not be such a total disaster."

"Up to you," he said. "I'm getting good money."

"And the prospect of more?"

"If I'm really lucky."

Russell was dining Pallant again but this time it wasn't boiled chicken and rice. They were eating in Russell's club in some state and Pallant was feeding almost normally. Charles Russell said: "I'm delighted it's better."

"My ulcer, you mean? I've almost forgotten it."

"I was hoping that when the pressure eased –"

"It's partly that and partly self-treatment. My doctor doesn't approve but it works. When it starts to play up I give it a solid meal to cope with. Wasn't there some old wives' wisdom in India that the way to deal with a tropical liver was to give it the hottest curry a Goan could make?"

"I've heard the story but never tried it. I didn't drink much in those days and my liver stood up. Anyway I'm delighted you're better."

'Delighted', he thought, was an understatement. If Pallant had

172

been obliged to retire, somebody would have had to replace him and that somebody would not have been Willy. But give Willy a few more years of experience, something of the *gravitas* which impressed politicians rather more than ability, and William Wilberforce Smith would have a chance.

Over coffee and brandy Charles Russell asked: "What's cooking in the shop at the moment?"

"Nothing explosive but the rats don't stop gnawing. Pinkos of all shades, some futile, some less so. Avant-garde philosophers, situation-ethics men ... And behind the soft-boiled eggs the hard ones. The dedicated and trained subversives behind the fronts which unlike FAAR are deliberate. And two of them are well-known charities."

"You don't sound optimistic."

"I'm not. The rats are going to win in the end."

"Then have a little more brandy while you still can."